Royal House of Leone

The PRINCESS

and the

PLAYER

by Jennifer Lewis

1

"You may be a widow, but you're not dead."

"I'm well aware of that." Carolina Leone didn't want to show her daughter how much her words stung. "I have a very full life." They walked along the Rue Faubourg Saint-Honoré in Paris, ostensibly looking for a birthday gift for her. Her scientist daughter, Callista, had been too busy to shop for one before now. "Running the palace is a full-time job, especially since your brother has moved into the castle in the village."

"Mom, you're not a building caretaker. And Dad's been gone for nearly a year now. You should go on a date." She winked one of her pretty green eyes.

"Lord, no." Lina almost shuddered. The prospect of dating again seemed as laughable as climbing Mt. Everest.

"I'm serious, you're still young, you're gorgeous, you have a lot to give. I'll be very ticked off if you wall yourself up in that palace and say goodbye to life."

"I have all of you to keep up with. Just traveling to visit my children all over the world could take most of the year."

Callista cocked her head, sending her auburn curls cascading over her shoulder. "Mom, you can't live through your children. And we're all busy."

Lina flinched. Was her daughter bored and annoyed by her presence here? She didn't think so, but still.... "I don't need a gift, darling. I have everything I want. Let me buy you lunch instead." She knew her daughter needed to get back to her lab.

"We could go to Carlo's," Callista turned down a side street. "I am hungry. We'll find you something awesome later." The sidewalk narrowed as they walked past a construction site. They had to pick their way past a pile of broken concrete, and at one point Lina put her hand out to steady herself on the temporary plywood wall.

The wall was covered in pasted posters for various events around the city, but when she saw the one her fingers rested on, she stopped and stared.

Amadou Khadem at The Olympia, May 10! His face stared right at her, dark eyes as intense and piercing as ever. *Tickets almost sold out!*

"Mom, are you okay?"

"Oh, yes, I'm fine." She dragged herself away from the poster with some effort. May tenth was tomorrow. But she'd never go see it. She didn't even remember the last time she'd been to a concert that wasn't a classical concerto.

But she couldn't resist sneaking one last look at the poster.

"Mom, what are you...? Hey, isn't it that guy you met once?"

"What?" Had she told Callista about him? She couldn't have—could she? Callista had a frighteningly good memory. She came out with stuff that no one else remembered.

"Yes, you said you met him long ago, before you had us. Before you met Dad, even. And look, the concert's tomorrow. Let's go see him."

"Oh, no. I don't think so." Panic surged through her. She couldn't even imagine being in the same space with him. Just seeing his face again was a shock. "It'll be too noisy."

"It's music, Mom, not noise. And I love his sound. It'll be fun."

"I'd really rather not." Thankfully Carlo's was only a few steps away, and soon she was able to fuss over whether to sit inside or out and whether to get an appetizer, and could drag her attention away from the man she'd had to work very—very—hard to forget all those years ago.

But that evening, alone in her hotel room— her daughter shared an apartment with two other female scientists and there was no spare bed—she pulled out her laptop and opened a browser.

It couldn't hurt just to look up his name and see what he'd been up to. Could it?

It had been years—decades—since she'd seen him. She was curious to see what Amadou looked like now, and the poster had been an

3

extreme close-up of his face so it was hard to get an overall impression.

She Googled his name. She'd always liked his name and the way it rolled off his tongue, in that deep, French-accented voice of his. He was probably here in Paris right now, with the concert so soon.

She glanced over her shoulder, as if suddenly afraid she was being watched. Which was silly, since there was *absolutely nothing* whatsoever wrong with what she was doing. He was an old friend. Not even a friend.

She clicked on the Wikipedia page at the top of her search, and her eyes darted to the right of the screen to see his personal details, wife, children, etc. And there were none, just his birthdate—he was a year older than her—and "years active" up to the present. Had he never been married? Never had children? It seemed impossible.

There was a recent picture of him performing live, standing at a mic, his face taut with emotion. A weird frisson of—something— swept through her as she studied it. He always had so much passion. Too much passion for normal life.

He did look different from the boy she remembered. In the picture he wore a sweat-dampened white T-shirt that outlined muscled shoulders and a hard chest. He'd been skinny and insubstantial when she knew him, barely eating and staying up all night. Now he had a muscled solidity that gave him an air of authority and confidence.

4

Of course, he'd always been confident. Infuriatingly so.

He didn't look like a man of fifty-four. If she'd had to guess, she'd have said maybe mid to late thirties. His hair was still dark, his brown skin was smooth and unlined, and his eyes sparkled with the same bold mischief she remembered.

Or maybe she just imagined that. The picture was too small to tell.

She let out a sigh. Goodness, he was handsome. Always had been. As a sheltered girl from the German countryside, she'd found him overwhelming and impossible to resist.

Of course she eventually came to her senses after her family arranged her meeting with Prince Emil and she'd got swept up in the majesty of Altaleone.

Amadou would have become bored with her and broken her heart, she knew it even then. And the fact that he'd never married confirmed it. He'd probably spent his whole life skipping from flower to flower, drinking their nectar like a gorgeous, confident bee they had no chance of refusing.

Her phone buzzed, and she quickly closed the web page before answering, as if she'd been caught doing something naughty.

"Mom, I got us tickets!"

"Tickets to what?" Her heart started pounding.

"Amadou Khadem, of course! Did you think I bought opera tickets? I got two right up front—the ones they save for industry bigwigs and VIPs. I think the guy in the box office recognized my name or something. Sometimes it's great being royal."

"That's wonderful, sweetheart." Her voice sounded flat. Her thoughts spun and a sudden surge of adrenaline propelled her to her feet. "You really didn't have to."

"Of course I didn't, but I need a night out as much as you do. I've barely been anywhere except to the lab for over a month. I have to attend an all-day conference tomorrow, but I'll pick you up at six."

"Great." Did her apprehension show in her voice? Usually the spotlights threw the crowd into darkness, but if the seats were right up front Amadou might be able to see her. Though even if he did see her he probably wouldn't recognize her after all these years. She was more than thirty years older and wore her hair differently. Maybe he'd wonder who that sweet old lady in the front row was.

"Mom, I need to finish up my Powerpoint for tomorrow, so I'll see you at six, okay?"

"Yes, dear, good luck tomorrow." Her children were so capable and confident that it often amazed her. How had they developed such a strong sense of self? Certainly not from her.

She'd always been somewhere in the background, smiling and supporting her husband. Maybe she should be embarrassed about it, but she'd really never wanted anything else.

She paced around the room, unable to settle.

Seeing Amadou—even on the poster—had opened up a window to a part of her she'd almost forgotten. Was it her heart? Maybe somewhere more primal. The part of her that could see a man and say, *wow*.

She hadn't felt the rush of attraction in...forever. She didn't even remember feeling it for Emil, and maybe she hadn't since their marriage was actually the brainchild of her well-connected relatives rather than a typical flirtation.

She had loved him, though, despite everything. She missed Emil's sense of humor, and the way he used to kiss her good night no matter what. Even after all these months it was still hard to believe he was gone forever. And there was no way she could embark on any kind of relationship with the eyes of European society and the world press on her every moment.

So any stray sparks of desire she felt would best be quickly extinguished.

"I'm so sorry I was late! The last speaker rambled on forever." Callista had grabbed a taxi from home and picked Lina up on the way so as not to deal with parking, and they'd jumped out, paid and were running into the theater a full hour after the concert was supposed to begin. "Do you think they'll let us in?"

"I don't know." Lina wasn't sure if she'd be relieved or crushed after all the time she'd spent trying to find an outfit that looked both hip and respectable at the same time. They'd probably missed him completely. "I suppose we can always play the royal card."

"I don't know if that works at gigs." Callista shot her a grin. "Might have the opposite effect."

They checked in at the box office, and the clerk told them to hurry. They'd missed the warm-up band and Amadou Khadem was about to play.

"Sweet!" Callista clapped her hands. "C'mon, Mom. We have to get all the way down to the front."

People frowned and peered at them as they walked past the cheap seats, then the medium-priced seats and then past the expensive seats and the very expensive seats, until they got to the front row, right in the middle. One rather rude man even demanded to see their tickets, refusing to believe that they could just waltz up to the front like this.

Callista ignored him, and they'd just managed to settle into their seats and remove their jackets when the band took their places, and an emcee walked toward the mic.

"Tonight, ladies and gentlemen"— Lina was almost fluent in French, so she understood him—"we welcome one of the most celebrated stars of the international music scene. He just finished a six-week tour of the U.S. and we're very lucky to have him here in Paris tonight. Here he is, the reigning king of desert soul—"

He turned to one of the wings and the drummer played a roll. Lina held her breath as a man emerged—not a myth or a legend and no larger than any other tall man—and walked toward the mic. She couldn't even see him, really, without the spotlight on his face. He wore a black jacket and pants and his hair was cropped short.

See? She could look right at him and barely react at all. This was going to be absolutely fine.

The emcee threw up his hands. "Amadou Khadem!"

The spotlight hit his face, throwing his bold features into high relief. Hard cheekbones, that proud nose and those eyes that seemed to see right through you.

He walked up to the mic. "I'm always glad to be back in Paris, my favorite city and spiritual homeland. I've missed you."

"We've missed you, too," intoned the woman next to her. Lina turned to look at her, then turned back to him, wondering why he wasn't speaking.

And as she turned their gaze locked, and she found herself staring right into the intense, dark eyes of the man she'd coolly left more than thirty years ago.

2

Is he looking at me? Lina wasn't sure if he could even see her past the harsh glare of the spotlight. As he launched into the first song, looking deep into the back of the audience, she wondered if she'd imagined the whole thing.

Soon the power of the music took hold of her, and she got swept along, enjoying his strong, melodic voice and paying as little attention as possible to the movements of his muscled body as he paced back and forth on the stage, pouring his heart into each song.

Such passion. He'd always had a lot of passion. Way too much for a quiet girl educated in a German boarding school.

He didn't look at her again either. No doubt she had imagined that moment of intense connection. She was just another face in a sea of them, and soon she would leave the concert with the crowd and not lay eyes on him again for another thirty years or so.

If even then. During the intermission she distracted herself with a glass of wine at the bar and annoyed Callista with questions about her own love life—which was apparently nonexistent.

She'd probably have said the same thing to her mother when she was that age.

The second half of the concert began with a fast-paced number that had much of the audience on their feet dancing. She stayed seated. She was in the front row and didn't want to block anyone's view.

Callista prodded her in midsong. "Mom, this guy's trying to give you something."

"What?" She turned to see a short, rotund man holding out a folded piece of paper.

"No, thank you." She tried to be polite. Whatever it was, she didn't want it.

"It's from Mr. Khadem," said the man, leaning in. He was blocking the view of the person next to her in the front row, and he was starting to look annoyed.

"Just take it, Mom," hissed Callista.

Amadou was still singing, and she didn't dare look up at him. But she took the note, totally forgetting to offer a polite acknowledgement.

She didn't want to open it and read it, either. The person next to her would be sure to wonder what it was that had been worth obscuring his view at an expensive concert. And if it really was from Amadou—which seemed unlikely—what would it say?

"Read it, Mom!" Callista looked ready to grab the note from her. "Or I will."

Her threat sent a jolt of panic through Lina. She might have mentioned an acquaintance with Amadou in passing at some point, but she'd definitely never told her about all the steamy summer nights she'd spent in his attic bedroom, or the long walks they'd shared in the mountains outside Zurich.

Even Emil never knew about her long affair with him. No one did, except her closest friends from school.

She cracked the note open and peered at it. Scrawled writing that she couldn't read. For one thing, it was dark. For another she needed reading glasses. She had some in her bag. Was she really going to reach into her bag for some old-lady reading glasses in front of the celebrated Amadou Khadem and his audience of devoted fans?

Apparently, yes. At this point she was committed. And what did she care if he thought she looked like a middle-aged woman? She was, wasn't she?

She fished out her glasses and put them on, then pulled the note to the right distance, and read it as fast as she could.

Please come up to my dressing room after the show.

She froze. Her eyes darted to him before she could stop them. Once again he stared straight at her—still singing—and held her gaze for a solid five seconds before she managed to tear it away.

He'd recognized her. Still, she didn't have to go. Really, it would be better not to. He'd only be disappointed anyway.

And heck, maybe he was still mad at her for the way she'd ended things. Back then she'd thought that everything she did during that strange in-between period of her life was temporary, disposable, soon to be forgotten, but it was funny how everything stuck with you over the years, whether you wanted it to or not.

Yes, it would definitely be better to leave. He'd probably decide that he'd mistaken her identity and she was just someone who bore an uncanny resemblance to the Carolina he once knew.

"What does it say?" Callista's whisper startled her.

"Oh, nothing."

Callista gave her a disbelieving look but went back to watching the concert.

Now Lina's heart was pounding. She barely dared look at Amadou's face and tried to distract herself by staring at the members of his band, or his hands moving over his instrument. Every song brought them closer to the end of the concert, when she planned to betray him for a second time by sneaking off without seeing him.

She should never have left Altaleone. At this hour she should be lying quietly in her bed in the palace, finishing that mystery novel with the missing cat.

Her agony dragged on as the concert appeared to end, then Amadou kept coming back for encores. The entire crowd was now on its feet, cheering, and she had to do the same so as not to stand out, though inside she was dying of embarrassment and misgivings and looking everywhere but at the tall, imposing man in the center of the stage, only a few yards from her face.

Finally—she'd begun to think it would never

happen—he exited and a big curtain closed and people started to gather their bags.

Thank goodness! She prodded Callista, who was putting on her jacket far too slowly. "Let's hurry. We don't want to get stuck in here."

"Mom, we're stuck anyway. We're way up front." The aisles had filled with people from the rows behind them. "Just relax. And tell me what that note said."

"I can't. We need to—" Panic surged through her as the short man materialized again, with a serious expression on his face.

"Please accompany me backstage. Mr. Khadem has invited you to his dressing room."

"Wow! Awesome!" Callista's thrilled exclamation would have made her jump if she wasn't frozen to the spot. "I wonder why? Could he have recognized you just from you meeting him before?"

"Uh…" Lina wracked her brain for a way to get out of this. If they went upstairs Callista would quickly find out that they'd done a whole lot more than meet. Her family had told Emil's that she was a virgin when they married, though luckily he'd had the decency never to even joke about it. Amadou could easily reveal that she was very far from being a virgin by the time she'd walked away from him.

And the way she'd done it. Her breath caught at the bottom of her lungs when she thought of the carefully typed letter she'd sent him. With no forwarding address. And he'd had the decency never to try to track her down. He must have known her crazy story was true when he saw the royal wedding pictures in the papers.

"C'mon, Mom, let's go." Callista pushed her forward. The man smiled, though it was a rather uncertain one, given her hesitation, and ushered them through the crowd off toward the side of the stage. "Isn't this exciting?" her daughter breathed, as he led them into the wings, where technicians and other staffers rushed around pulling cords and packing up instruments.

Lina couldn't gather enough sensible thoughts to respond. What would Amadou say when he saw her? Was he still angry? Or did he just think of her as an old friend? Really old. With reading glasses and a silver streak in her blonde hair.

They passed through a cluttered corridor, then up to a door with a crowd of people gathered outside. Their guide muttered something in French, and the crowd parted. Lina held her breath as they headed into the dressing room under the gaze of his entourage.

Amadou sat in a chair facing away from them, wiping his face with a towel. His shirt was drenched with perspiration and clung to his muscled shoulders. Lina wanted to blush at catching him so unprepared, but as soon as his man spoke, he sprang to his feet, dropped the towel and pressed his hands around hers.

She must have stuck her hand out to shake or something. She wasn't even sure. "Hi," she stammered, trying to act like she wasn't about to explode. How did he still look so young? He didn't even look ten years older than when she'd last seen him. Darker-skinned people often did age better. And barely a sprinkle of gray hair. She could see the silver more in the stubble on his hard chin.

Still so handsome.

She cursed that thought and tried to pack it off to some unused recess of her brain. He still hadn't spoken yet. He stared at her face as if unable to believe his eyes.

Probably shocked by how different she looked. A matronly mother of ten. She'd never have predicted it herself.

"My God, Carolina." He squeezed her hand. She could feel emotion roll off him, or maybe it was just heat. The dressing room was hot and filled with nervous energy, probably from the exhausting and exhilarating performance. "My God."

Wow, this was the most awkward exchange ever. All her years of diplomatic training hadn't prepared her for this. "The performance was wonderful." Her attempt at appropriate speech came out sounding clipped and forced.

He stared at her for a moment longer, then, still holding tight to her hand, let out a loud laugh that shocked her and almost made her jump.

She felt like such a phony. Heck, she was a professional phony. It was her job to smile and make polite conversation with people she would just as soon never see again.

At last he released his grip on her hand, and it shook as she took it back.

"I was so sorry to hear about your husband." His deep measured voice sounded sincere. "A terrible tragedy."

"Yes. We hope to bring the killers to justice." This was getting more awkward by the second. Then she remembered her daughter! "This is my daughter Callista. She lives and works here in Paris."

Now he seized Callista's hand in both of his, then brought it to his lips and kissed it. Callista looked like she was about to pass out with delight. Luckily, he let her daughter have her hand back right away. "I'm so pleased to meet you. I can see you have your mother's beauty."

Callista wasn't usually the blushing type, but her cheeks grew pink. Lina wanted to laugh. She'd probably looked much the same the first time Amadou swept her off her feet with his practiced charm. "I've been a huge fan of yours for years. I have all your albums."

"She bought our tickets as a birthday present for me," offered Lina, keen to offer an innocuous conversational gambit. She didn't want him thinking it was her idea to come here tonight.

"Today is your birthday?" He frowned at Lina. "No. Your birthday is Tuesday. May ninth."

"I can't believe you remember." Uh-oh, they were wading into dangerous territory here. "It's been a long time. More than thirty years."

Callista's expression revealed that she'd figured out they were more than acquaintances. "How exactly do you two know each other?"

A slow smile tilted one corner of Amadou's expressive mouth. "It's a long story. Perhaps we can tell it to your daughter over dinner?"

"No!" the word shot out of Lina's mouth. "I mean, it's late. She has a big meeting tomorrow."

"Just you, then. My favorite restaurant is only steps away, and I'm always starving after a concert. I'll be deeply offended if you don't join me." Just enough humor shone in his dark eyes to suggest—at least to others—that he was joking.

But she knew he wasn't joking. If she turned him down, she'd give him yet another reason to never forgive her.

"Go on, Mom. You can walk back to your hotel afterward. It's so close."

"I'll escort your mother back safely," assured Amadou, already looking confident. "Just give me a few moments to change. Mustafa, please look after Mme. Leone while I shower." He disappeared into an anteroom. This might have been a good moment to make a speedy exit if it weren't for Mustafa and the still-gathered throng now talking among themselves in more than one language.

Trapped, she made awkward conversation about nothing with Callista and smiled grimly at Mustafa, who looked very suspicious of her and the whole situation. As well he might.

In less than two minutes Amadou emerged dressed in black pants and a bright white shirt, also slightly damp but this time with fresh water from the shower. He toweled off his hair and looked relieved that she was still there.

This was so weird, being backstage while he

showered. Far too intimate. He never had been the type to stand on ceremony, but still. He pulled on some sharp-looking leather shoes and placed a dark fedora onto his head. Then he extended his arm.

Lina gulped, then took it. How could she not?

Callista stared. Lina could tell that her daughter would have stayed up all night and missed her meeting if she thought for even one second that she'd be welcome at this dinner. But she knew she wasn't, and so did everyone else there.

Amadou had claimed her.

Again.

3

The restaurant he took her to was less than two blocks away and totally invisible from the street. They entered through a large carriage door into a tidy cobbled courtyard—like so many buildings in Paris—with just four tables set for dinner. A couple and a laughing group of four were the only customers.

"This looks rather exclusive," she murmured, more to make conversation than anything else.

"It's the best. I come here every time I'm in town." His gaze lingered, as if he still couldn't quite believe she was right here with him.

The maître d' led them to a table, and she removed her jacket while the waiter poured water and Amadou ordered wine.

"I'm surprised you recognized me."

"Why? You're in the social pages of the papers quite often."

"You read the social pages?"

A wry smile crossed his mouth. "Only to catch a glimpse of you."

"I don't believe it for a minute. You're far too busy. You seem to spend each year circling the globe and performing on every continent except Antarctica."

"I performed in Antarctica two years ago. For the scientists." His cheek creased as he grinned. She'd always loved his smile, so quick and warm. That hadn't changed. "Of course I mostly went because I wanted to see the place."

"You always loved to travel. Do you have a home base these days?"

"This is it." He gestured around them.

"This restaurant?" She sipped her wine.

He laughed. "No, this city. Paris. It's where I grew up, remember."

"I didn't know you back then. And you didn't talk about it much." He'd seemed kind of bitter about his life back then and—young and shallow—she hadn't wanted to hear depressing details about his impoverished childhood. She was more interested in the dynamic musician he'd blossomed into. "It's great that you're still performing after all these years. Do you know how unusual that is?"

"And you're still royal after all these years. That's rather offbeat, too."

"We always did dream big." She smiled, then wondered if she'd said the wrong thing. Becoming a royal wife was hardly something one aspired to. That sounded tacky. Though probably no one married a future king by mistake either.

"Your husband never became king "

"No. His mother was still going strong when they were killed. He didn't mind not being king. He wasn't too interested in pomp and ceremony. He liked to focus on hunting and the vineyards. He enjoyed his life, short as it was."

"With you at his side, how could he not?" Amadou lifted his freshly poured glass of wine. "*Salut.*"

She raised her glass and sipped, then resolved to drink as little wine as possible. She didn't want to get tipsy around this man. He already had a dangerously intoxicating effect on her.

He'd removed his fedora so she could see his face clearly. His brow was smooth and unlined—the face of a man with a clear conscience. A man who enjoyed his life. "You look happy."

"I am happy. I make sure of it." He smiled slowly, his gaze wandering over her face. "I wish I could say the same for you."

She felt an awkward expression pass over her face. "I'm happy! Very happy." Her words sounded rushed, forced. "I mean, of course I miss my husband. And my children are all grown and busy with their lives, so I'm in a transitional phase, but—"

"I understand. I didn't mean to accuse you of anything. Sometimes I'm too frank."

"You always were. You never could keep your opinion to yourself. Remember when you told that huge bouncer he was an ass because he wouldn't let you perform outside his club?"

"And he picked me up by the front of my shirt and hurled me against the wall." He laughed. "And he only held back from punching me because you begged him to."

"Exciting times." She laughed, too. Though she hadn't laughed at the time. She'd cried and been angry with him for being too rash. "Too exciting for me, really."

"Is that why you left me?" His question, on the tail of their laughter, was so serious, so clear and bold, that she knew he wanted a real answer.

She sighed. "I left because I was done with school and my family had other plans for me."

"You could have defied them."

"That's not who I am."

"You're very loyal." His eyes glittered. "To them, not to me."

"They were my family." Had she even thought about arguing with them? Not really. She'd always known her interlude with Amadou was just that—an exciting adventure that would have to end so her real life would begin.

She half expected him to accuse her of weakness and braced herself for defense.

"Family is important." He held his glass, not drinking but peering over it at her. "The happiest day of my life was when I finally bought my mother the house she'd always dreamed of. She still lives there. It's in the countryside outside Paris."

"That's wonderful. She must be so proud of you."

He shrugged. "She wishes I would settle down."

"And why don't you? You must be a wealthy man by now."

He laughed, but the laughter didn't reach his eyes. "Everyone always asks that sooner or later."

"You don't want to settle down. Is that why you never married?" As soon as the words left her mouth, she regretted them and wished she could take them back. Who was she to ask such a personal question?

"It's part of it. I can't settle down. It's not in me. I'm a nomad by heritage and inclination."

She wanted to argue that his mom presumably shared his nomadic heritage yet she was apparently happily settled in France.

But she knew better. She'd always been good at knowing what not to say. The skill came in handy in the social circles she moved in. "So you spend most of the year on the road."

"It's what I love best. So of course we could never have been together for long. You had dreams of castles and a large family, and I had dreams of the road." He sounded like he was trying to convince himself.

She nodded. "True. All good things must come to an end." She uttered the platitude just wanting to agree with him and smooth the conversation.

But he didn't reply. And his silence stretched out until an awkward space for thought opened up. A space that echoed with the words "what if?"

"We should order." She wanted to fill the air with sound, though they'd barely glanced at their menus. "I think I'll have the boeuf en croute."

"A very traditional choice." His comment sounded slightly scolding.

She rose to the bait. "I am a very traditional girl."

His mouth hitched into a half smile. "Yes. You always were, deep down. I suppose that was one of the things that attracted me to you. I shouldn't have been so surprised when you walked away from a poor street musician to marry a prince."

"Were you really surprised?" She hadn't let herself think too much about how he would feel. The end was always written into their relationship—at least for her—and she'd assumed he felt the same.

He stared at her long enough to make her heart pound. Then his eyes narrowed slightly and flashed with unexpected emotion. "I was devastated."

4

Amadou leaned back in his chair, appraising the effect of his admission.

He'd silenced her. Did she really think she was just another notch on his bedpost?

She had the decency to look shocked for a moment. Then she laughed. A polite tinkle of a laugh. The kind of laugh you'd trot out at a royal tea party. "You're teasing me."

"If only I were." He let his words sit in the air for a moment. Just long enough to make her uncomfortable.

Why did he want to make her uncomfortable? All of this was so long ago even he had almost forgotten it. Until he saw her face in the first row of his audience. Then something had roared back to life inside him with fearsome power that threatened to unman him.

"I should have known you were out of reach," he said at last, after she'd reached nervously for her wine glass. "But I never was one to accept any limits in myself or others. Naïve, I suppose."

"You seemed so worldly to me. I thought I was the naïve one."

"I guess we were both wrong." Looking at her right now, he could almost taste the cherry apple flavor of her mouth. Amazing that he still remembered it after all these years. He wondered if she'd taste the same.

He wanted to find out.

"I guess it's lucky you'd seen my picture in the papers. I must look so different." She touched her elegantly coiffed hair. It looked like it had been set by a stylist. Maybe she had one come to her room every morning.

"In some ways you do." He let his gaze wander over her hair—not a strand out of place—and across the elegant planes of her face. "You look more...established."

"Matronly." Her quiet exclamation startled him. "It's okay. I know I do. You can't have ten children and not look matronly." A pink flush appeared above her cheekbones.

"Nonsense. You look calm, quietly at home in the world. When you were younger you always acted like you were in a big rush to get somewhere. But matronly? No way." He let his gaze drift lower, to the swell of her breasts, the lovely body emphasized by the elegant lines of her expensive pantsuit.

She'd lost that breathless air of excitement she always had about her, but in its place glowed something deeper, warmer, and he wanted to bask in its glow.

He wanted to peel away her cleverly designed layers and run his fingers through her artfully styled hair. He wanted to explore the redrawn continent of her body and lose himself in both

27

its known and its unexpected mountains and rivers.

She shifted, uncomfortable, and he realized he was staring like a teenage boy who'd never seen a woman before. Luckily, the waiter arrived to take their order, which provided enough distraction for him to pull himself together.

Carolina.

For years he'd smarted from her sudden and totally unexpected departure. And now here she was, within reach.

At least for as long as it took her to eat her way through her boeuf en croute. "Are you in Paris for long?"

"Just until next week."

He wanted exact details but didn't want to spook her by pressing for them. "You're here to spend time with your daughter?"

"Yes, and to do some shopping. It probably sounds crazy, but I often do Christmas shopping at this time of year. With so many children I like to take my time and not end up in a mad rush."

"I'm surprised you do it yourself. You probably have people for that."

"To buy presents for my children? Why would I want someone else to do that? It's fun." Her warm smile lit up something inside him. "I get sad when I've finally bought enough."

"You could buy presents for poor children." He wasn't sure why he said that. Maybe he wanted to scold her for being so rich and content as well as beautiful and unattainable.

"I do." She looked earnest. "I always buy

28

presents for the poor children in Altaleone."

"I'm surprised there are any."

She shrugged and smiled. "There aren't many. But someone's always falling through a crack somewhere. Parents with drug or alcohol problems or who are going through some kind of crisis. And we've taken in quite a few refugees in the past few years, just like everywhere else."

"It's kind of you to think of others." He mouthed the empty words, thinking about how much he'd like to kiss her full mouth.

She laughed. "You don't have to patronize me."

Her comment shocked him. "I didn't mean to." Or did he? Neither of them was eating the bread the waiter had placed on the table. The distraction of her presence—so enchanting and unexpected—had stolen his appetite for food.

While dangerously inflaming other appetites he preferred not to think of.

"What do you do for fun these days?" she asked.

"Perform," he answered honestly. "I never get tired of sharing my music with a crowd of people and watching them respond.

"But when you're not onstage. What do you do?"

"I enjoy whatever city I'm in." He liked to maintain the illusion that he was an easygoing playboy. No one but his tiny inner circle knew what he really got up to when the lights were off. That he had a whole other vocation unrelated to music. Everything went more smoothly that way, and fewer lives were put at risk. "If I weren't with you I'd probably be hitting a jazz club with my drummer and my bassist."

"Do you still stay up to watch the dawn?" Her slim eyebrow lifted. She'd always teased him about being such a night owl.

"More often than I care to admit."

"You never were normal."

"More's the pity. If I was, then maybe you wouldn't have left me." He was teasing her. They both knew she would have left him anyway.

"Do your girlfriends mind you moving around so much?"

"Yes," he admitted. "My nomadic lifestyle has broken up a lot of relationships. Why do ladies always want to settle down somewhere?"

"It's our nesting instinct. We want to build a home and fill it with children. I don't think any mother wants to spend her life herding children on and off planes and trying to find meals they'll eat in a strange city where she doesn't speak the language."

He laughed. "I suppose I can see that."

"Did you ever have children?" She asked cautiously. She probably knew the answer. At least if she'd read about him at all over the years, the way he had looked up news about her. Maybe she hadn't bothered.

"No."

"You always said you wouldn't, so I guess you kept your promise."

"You though I was crazy."

"I suppose I still do." She crinkled her nose

in a really cute way. "I don't understand it. A lot of men don't want children when they're young like we were, but most do eventually."

"Not me." He shrugged. "Too much responsibility. I float better when I'm not tied down." He had his pat line. He'd used it enough over the years. He even used it on his own mother.

Luckily, people had mostly stopped asking as he got older. And a vasectomy in his twenties had defused any claims of paternity that girls threw his way. He hadn't been a monk. "My songs are my children. They follow me everywhere and grow and change along with me."

"That's a cute metaphor. I guess they don't go off to college and get big, important jobs and leave you rattling around in an old palace with too many bedrooms."

He grinned. "Not yet, anyway."

The waiter brought their food way too fast. *Uh-oh.* And the portions at these fancy Paris restaurants were annoyingly tiny. They'd be finished in about two minutes. Perhaps he could convince her to get dessert. Or maybe go to a club with him. He didn't want to stop talking to her.

"My daughter Callista was so thrilled to meet you." Her smile lit up her face.

"Did you tell her about you and me?" He assumed he'd been kept as a dark secret over the years.

"Oh, no. She has no idea. I told her that we met once." She laughed, no doubt oblivious to the knife she drove into his heart.

Of course she hadn't told anyone. A nearly yearlong affair with a street musician from the bottom rung of society was hardly something you'd brag about to your royal family. They all probably thought she was still a virgin, fresh from her fancy Swiss finishing school. She'd made him laugh so hard with her stories about her classes in how to manage your servants and how many courses to serve at a state dinner.

Obviously they'd come in more useful over the years than anything he'd taught her.

"Maybe you could sign an autograph for her?"

"I'd be happy to. We can go back to my hotel and pick out a souvenir for her."

The look of alarm that crossed her face told him he'd stepped waaaay out of line. "Or I could bring something to you tomorrow." He spoke fast. "I always keep a box of whatever they're selling at the venues. Would she like a T-shirt? A CD?" He felt like a traveling salesman, but this was his opportunity to see her again.

"Oh, I don't want to be any trouble. It would be great if you'd sign the program from tonight's concert." She fished a slightly crumpled program out of her purse. And a pen.

His heart sank. He felt like she'd asked him to sign his death warrant. There was something so final about giving her his autograph—as soon as he'd signed it, and paid the bill, they'd part ways and he wouldn't see her again for another thirty years.

He couldn't let that happen.

5

Lina watched Amadou hesitate about signing the program. "You don't have to. I suppose everyone's worried about fraud these days. You probably don't want anyone having your signature."

"I'm not worried. I use a different signature for autographs than I do for signing checks." He signed it. She watched his dark, bold scrawl cover half the front photo. "I'd just like to give her something more special."

"She'll be thrilled with this." She admired the signed program before tucking it back in her purse. "And now she'll probably pepper me with questions about how I really knew you."

"Will you answer them truthfully?"

"Probably not." A wry smile tugged at her mouth. "I don't want to shock her."

"She's a young woman. I doubt she'd be shocked. You might be surprised at what she gets up to when she'd not under your motherly gaze."

"True! I've always been careful not to try to control my children. I raised them to make wise decisions, but they're adults now and can make their own choices."

She managed to keep the conversation about his tours and which cities he liked best until the waiter removed their plates and asked if they'd like to hear the dessert menu.

"Oh, no, thanks," she said quickly. "I really should get going. It's been lovely." Things had gone smoothly so far, but being around Amadou made her nervous, like a powder keg was about to explode. She couldn't wait to get back to the quiet safety of her hotel room.

"How about a coffee?" asked Amadou softly.

"I can't drink coffee at this time of night. I won't sleep a wink."

Sadness flickered in his eyes. She was flattered that he wanted to spend more time with her, but that just wasn't a good idea.

"I'll be in Paris for two more weeks. I'd love to see you again." He looked relaxed on the outside, but his voice had an edge to it, an intensity that only spurred her desire to flee like Cinderella after the ball.

"Uh, maybe. My daughter has organized an awful lot of—"

"Can I text you my number?"

Goodness. This was getting way too intimate. Giving someone her personal phone number felt almost like giving them a key to her home. She usually gave people the main palace number, which was answered by a receptionist, but she could hardly do that with Amadou. "Uh, sure." He pulled out his phone, and she gave him her number. It wouldn't matter, really. He was always traveling. She'd soon be safely tucked away in the ancient cloisters of Altaleone.

She heard her phone ping as he texted her, but she resisted the urge to look at it. She gave him one of her polite ceremonial smiles instead, as she put on her jacket.

He rose and pulled out her chair, then donned his hat. She'd always loved how tall he was. Emil was only a couple of inches taller than her. Amadou towered over her, and she'd liked the way his sheer size made her feel safe.

Right now, however, she felt anything but safe. They exited the restaurant courtyard into the street and started the short walk toward her hotel, murmuring pleasantries about Paris at night.

Would they shake hands? Maybe hug? People didn't really hug members of the royal family, but then Amadou was hardly your average, everyday guy.

"This is it." She paused just before the brightly lit facade of the hotel. She didn't want to say goodbye in front of a phalanx of night porters and bellhops. "I'd better head in."

Before she had a chance to walk off, he took her gently in his arms and held her close. She could feel his fingertips press lightly into her back through the thin fabric of her jacket. Something swelled in her chest. It felt wonderful to be held by him again, for just a few moments.

"You haven't changed at all," he murmured.

"Oh, but I have." She pulled back just enough to look into his face. "Sometimes it's hard to believe I'm even the same person."

His warm dark gaze made her breath catch.

"I can hardly believe I'm holding you in my arms again." And before she had time to breathe—or protest—his lips captured hers in a kiss so tender that she thought her heart might burst.

Uh-oh. We're kissing. Her brain struggled to process a sudden barrage of information. Her body had no such difficulty. She simply melted into his arms, drawing closer to him and inhaling his spicy male scent. Memories swept over her like a gust of hot wind, spinning her back to a time when anything was possible.

He probably only kissed her for a couple of seconds before pulling back. "I've missed you, Lina."

I've missed you, too. She couldn't say it. She'd been married to someone else the whole time! She'd never be unfaithful to the memory of her dead husband by admitting that from time to time—hardly ever, really—she'd allowed herself to think back to those magical days and nights with Amadou.

"I'm glad we met again." She congratulated herself on a response that was both diplomatic and appropriately enthusiastic. She tugged herself gently from his embrace, feeling a tiny sense of loss as his muscled arms moved back to his sides.

"Me, too." She could tell that he wanted to say more and prayed he wouldn't. This was awkward enough already.

"Bye." She backed away, almost ready to turn and run.

"Goodbye, Carolina. I'll be in touch." He

kept his gaze on her, steady and unnerving, until she finally did turn and march toward the lobby with almost undignified speed. Had the hotel staff seen her kiss him?

She glanced around quickly. What if there were paparazzi nearby? Possibly she was being paranoid and no one really cared what some middle-aged dowager from an obscure microstate got up to, but if someone more exciting was staying here they might well be staked outside and anything that happened was fair game for their prying lenses.

"Good evening, madame." The doorman greeted her. She managed to nod a polite greeting back, while her mind spun so fast she hoped she wouldn't trip on the marble steps. "I trust you had a pleasant night out?"

Was he leering? Had he recognized Amadou? He was far more famous than her. She'd just die if her children found out about this. They'd be so shocked. Their father was dead barely a year.

She realized that she hadn't answered the doorman, who was now holding the door for her. "Lovely, thank you." Another ceremonial smile. If she could just get to her room without having to talk to anyone, that would be fantastic. Then she could scream—silently, of course— and release the tension building up inside her like a tsunami.

As she marched across the lobby, she heard her phone ping. Another text. She didn't dare look at it as she pressed the elevator button, then stepped in and pressed her floor.

By the time she got to her hotel room and let

herself inside, she'd already started to mistrust her memories. How could she have kissed him? She was a widow and still in mourning. She had a royal reputation to uphold and couldn't just go around kissing celebrity musicians if she felt like it.

Maybe the kiss was a figment of her underused imagination? Perhaps he'd given her a peck goodbye and she'd somehow reinvented it into a full-on smooch?

No. Impossible. Her lips still tingled, and her heartbeat skipped and jumped around. She could still feel the press of his strong fingers into her back.

She'd definitely kissed him and it had left an indelible mark on her psyche.

His text! She remembered it and pulled out her phone. First he'd texted her with just his name—so she'd know who the strange number belonged to. The second text took her a moment to unravel.

Be happy for this moment. This moment is your life.

Huh?

It was probably a quote from someone. When she'd been close to him, Amadou was always reading this and that, too impatient for formal education yet hungry for wisdom beyond his years.

She Googled the line and found it was from Omar Khayyam, a tenth-century Persian poet and mathematician. Typical! She had to smile. If this moment was her life, it was certainly unexpected.

Perhaps he'd sent her the text to forestall the regret he knew she'd feel as soon as she was alone with some common sense.

Her phone rang and she jumped. Surely he wasn't calling already?

No. It was Callista. She hesitated, wondering if she could pretend she'd already gone to bed.

Now you're going to fib to your children? You have nothing to hide! She picked it up. "Hello, darling. You really should be asleep."

"How can I sleep when I know my mom is out on a date with Amadou Khadem? I want *all* the details."

"Don't be silly, my love. We had a nice dinner, and now I'm back in my room."

"Is he there?"

"Callista!"

"You know I'm just kidding. It's just that I've never thought of you before with anyone other than Dad. And Amadou is just so…different from Dad."

"Yes. He was always very exciting. Too exciting."

"And that's why you left him for Dad?"

"Maybe. I don't remember. It was all so long ago."

"I had no idea you were such a woman of mystery. I suppose I thought you incubated at a strict boarding school for years, then walked right into a royal marriage. How did you ever even meet him?"

"We met by the lake in Zurich. He was playing his saxophone for tips from passersby—busking I think they call it—and he stopped playing to talk to me. I don't even know why I stopped to respond. I suppose he's not the type of person you can ignore."

"He was busking? That's hilarious. I cannot picture the international superstar performing for loose change."

"He was young. It wasn't such a strange thing to do in those days. One of my German girlfriends used to play her violin there, too." Now she was defending him. She didn't want Callista to see him as some kind of street hustler. He'd been mesmerizing even back then, always with a crowd around him. They'd all known it was only a matter of time before he hit it big.

"And I guess you guys became quite...intimate."

"We were friends. It was different back then. People didn't jump into bed with each other the way they do now." She should check the mirror to see if her nose was growing because that was a stone-cold lie! Though she hadn't jumped into bed with him until at least their third date.

"From the way he reacted to seeing you again I'd have thought you were a lot more than just friends. When are you seeing him again?"

"Again? Oh, no. It was just a friendly catch-up dinner. He's touring. I probably won't see him again for years."

She heard the sound of a text coming in. And ignored it.

"It's about time you started dating."

"Callista!"

"It's been a year. No one will hold it against you. I, for one, think you should get out and about more."

"That's why I came to Paris, remember?"

"Then I guess it's working." They wished each other good night. Goodness, it was late! Well after midnight. She undressed and removed her makeup. Then she remembered the newest text.

It could wait until morning. Already she was frazzled and overstimulated by the day's events. She really was happiest when she was pottering about in her rose garden, annoying the gardener with her suggestions.

But as she lay down in bed she realized it could be a text from one of the children. Or news in the case of her husband's murder. She picked up her phone and glanced at it.

I'm thinking about you.

Of course it was him. Who else would send a bold message like that to her phone?

She grabbed her phone and texted back quickly. **I'm a widow and still in mourning. I am thinking about my dead husband.** She sent it before she could second-guess herself.

In the silence that followed she had opportunity for regret. Did she have to be so brusque about it? Still, it annoyed her that he would flirt with her on such a short reacquaintance. He didn't know anything about her life between now and then.

Her phone pinged again, and she fought the urge to read it. And failed.

You are still alive. And more lovely than ever.

Flatterer! She cursed the smile that flew to

her lips. He could have probably taken half of the women in the audience out to dinner if he'd wanted to, but he'd wanted to be with her.

I want to see you tomorrow.

I already have plans. She texted back before she could think about the possibilities. She wasn't ready to start dating.

Forget dating—her being seen to be involved with Amadou would mean a media circus. She could just imagine the headlines. She wasn't ready for that either. The gaudy press coverage of the murders had only just died down, and she was relieved that they'd never uncovered the whole story of the compromising positions the bodies had been found in.

And she hoped they never would.

Cancel them. I'll pick you up first thing in the morning.

What? The nerve!

No. I need to sleep now. Goodbye.

Hopefully that was terse enough to discourage him.

Dead yesterdays and unborn tomorrows. Why fret about them, if today be sweet?

Another quote, no doubt. Probably Omar Khayyam again. She put her phone on her bedside table, determined not to respond.

The dead yesterdays were alarming enough, but the unborn tomorrows scared the heck out of her. Especially if any of them had the dangerously seductive Amadou Khadem in them...which she strongly suspected they would.

6

Will you meet me for lunch? He sent the message barely after seven-thirty a.m. Just couldn't wait any longer.

Sorry, I can't. I have plans.

Damn.

He wanted to push for more details, to ramp up and ask for dinner. Maybe even just to show up at her hotel and offer to escort her wherever she was going.

But he knew that if he came on too strong—which arguably he'd already done—he'd drive her away. If he played too safe, she'd slip out of his grasp. Amadou was no stranger to seducing women, but Carolina was a special challenge.

He stopped halfway through his morning series of sun salutations. Normally he used the yoga poses to focus on his breathing and clear his mind. Today his mind was cluttered—burdened—with thoughts of Carolina and how badly he wanted to see her again.

He resolved to go for a run instead and laced up his running shoes, then headed outside. A light drizzle blurred the air, and its cold drops on his face pulled him out of his overactive

43

imagination and into a reality with slippery streets and irritable commuters.

But it didn't slow his pace as he covered the distance between his hotel near the Champs-Elysées and hers near Boulevard Haussmann. He ran right past her hotel. Why did he want her so much, anyway?

It had been more than thirty years. He was over her. Or at least he'd thought he was. He was here in Paris on important business—the business of saving young lives from a grim fate. He didn't have time to lose his head over a woman. Especially this woman.

But a pit of longing still yawned somewhere deep inside him, cavernous enough to fuel his creativity and give his music depth and soul. If he actually did hook up with her and forge an impossible-to-imagine happy ending of sorts, perhaps it would kill all his creative urges and leave him a happy and empty shell with no music in him.

He shuddered. Better to be alone with his music.

Right?

Maybe that wasn't it anyway. He stopped and glanced back down the street behind him, past the spot where he'd kissed her last night. He'd known the kiss would be unexpected, unwelcome, even. Maybe that was why he'd done it. Perhaps he wanted revenge for the way she'd coldly walked away from him when he'd thought they were so close.

Clearly their relationship had meant a lot less to her than it had to him. They'd never discussed the future but who did at twenty? They didn't even think beyond the next week at that age. He hadn't questioned where their union was going, hadn't even thought about it until he got that crisp, apologetic letter.

He did deserve a little revenge for that. He'd burned the letter that night, but its words were seared into his brain. *I enjoyed our time together.* Like they'd just shared a pleasant evening! *I wish you much success.* As if he needed her good wishes or anyone else's. He'd always known he was going to make it and sooner rather than later.

He turned away and started running again, determination rippling in his veins.

He was going to bed Carolina Leone.

"Uh, no, don't come up. I'll come down." Lina didn't want her daughter entering her room and seeing the three big vases of flowers Amadou had sent her. Since their kiss two days ago he'd texted her several times with invitations and she'd turned them all down.

And now the flowers? Why? He must know by now that she didn't want to see him again.

Well, she did, but she knew it was a terrible idea and that she absolutely MUST NOT DO IT.

Surely he'd received the hint by now? Would she have to come out and tell him that she wouldn't see him again no matter what?

He'd *done* something to her. She wasn't sure if it happened with the kiss or sometime before. Maybe even while she was watching him during his concert. Something was different inside her—in her brain and her body. She hadn't felt true arousal for years. It pained her to admit that she'd lost those feelings for her husband at least a decade ago. She felt deep affection for him but none of the zing that had accompanied their caresses in the early years of their marriage.

Yes, she'd done her duty in the bedroom, but she hadn't fully enjoyed it for a long time. She'd assumed her lack of interest was due to normal changes in the body and brain due to growing older. Really, it would be distasteful if older people wandered around pawing at each other the way young ones did.

Wouldn't it?

And now suddenly she had all those awkward, uncomfortable, hot, sticky feelings pulsing and churning inside her like she was twenty again. It was undignified and downright disturbing!

The last thing she needed was to find herself in close proximity to the man who'd jump-started her rusting motor.

Where was her lipstick? She searched the bathroom, then looked on the dressing room table. Perhaps it was in her handbag? She hadn't been outside without lipstick on in decades, and there was press everywhere in Paris. It was her royal duty to look the part at all times.

She knelt down and peered under the bed. Yes! The gold tube gleamed in the shadows. It must have fallen and been kicked under there. She reached an arm in and—

A knock on the door made her jump.

"Who is it?"

"It's me, Mom, let me in."

"I told you to wait downstairs."

"I know. Do I always listen to you?"

"I'll be out in a minute." She grabbed the lipstick and climbed to her feet, heart pounding. She had to get out of there without Callista seeing the flowers. She hadn't been able to think of a way to get rid of them without drawing attention. It was awkward to ask housekeeping to remove them.

She patted her hair back into place and headed for the door. If she could just slip out and— She pulled on the handle and tried to ease her way through the open crack.

"Not so fast. I came up because I need to use the bathroom."

"There's one in the lobby."

"There's a closer one up here. Do you have a man hiding in there or something?" Callista lifted a brow. "You're up to something! What's going on?"

"Nothing's going on," insisted Lina, upset that she already looked and sounded guilty when she hadn't actually done anything at all.

"Then let me in."

Reluctantly she stepped aside and let her daughter in. "It's a mess. The maid didn't come yet."

"What beautiful flowers!" Callista made a beeline for them. She grabbed the tag. Lina closed her eyes and cursed herself for not removing it.

"Whoa, these are from Amadou Khadem? Mom! What's going on here? Are you having an affair with him?" Her daughter's eyes were wide as saucers.

"I most certainly am not."

"Then why is he sending you flowers?" She picked up the card on the next vase. At least he'd had the common sense not to write anything compromising in his notes. Each one simply said "To Carolina, from Amadou."

"Three bouquets?" She picked up the third tag. "Have you seen him again?"

"No." She sighed. "He's asked me out several times. I wish he'd stop."

"Why? He's dreamy. Do you think he'd notice if I went instead?"

"Let's see, age difference aside, I'm blonde sprinkled with silver and have blue eyes and you have curly chestnut hair and green eyes."

"Men aren't all that observant." Callista winked. "Seriously, though. He must be kind of crazy about you."

Lina shrugged. "I'm not really sure what's going on in his mind. But I know my own mind. I'll always be your father's wife and that's that."

"Mom! You can't just wall yourself up in Dad's tomb. You have a lot of life to live. You should at least be open to dating."

"Why? So I can get my heart broken in public by a famous musician? The paparazzi are merciless. You know what they did to Princess Diana right here in Paris."

"That was years ago."

"And you really think things are different? If I went on a date—especially with someone famous like him—I'd be opening myself up to be preyed on by vultures. I'd rather stay home with a good book."

Callista sighed. "You do have a point. But maybe some quiet country gentleman could work? Someone respectable, who the paparazzi wouldn't care about."

"Someone nice and dull who collects claret and lives to shoot ducks and hunt rare mushrooms." Lina had to laugh.

"Exactly."

"Like I said, I'd prefer a good book. Are you going to use the bathroom, or are we just going to stand here all morning? I want to see the Renoir exhibit before it gets too crowded."

"Won't be a minute." Callista vanished into the bathroom, and Lina ripped the cards off the flowers and threw them in the bin. If anyone else waltzed in here, at least they wouldn't know she was under siege by Amadou. And what did he want with her, anyway?

He probably just wanted to break her heart as revenge for her carelessly breaking his all those years ago.

Her phone pinged. **If you'll have dinner with me I'll stop sending flowers.**

She had to laugh. Maybe it would be worth it. She could have dinner with him and tell him—to his face—exactly how she felt and that their kiss had been a one-off mistake and that they were both grown-ups with completely incompatible lives and—

On that condition, I will have dinner with you.

Her thumb pressed send before she could

retract it.

I'll pick you up in your lobby at eight.

Adrenaline surged through her at the thought of people seeing them together. **Can we meet somewhere more private?**

Of course. I'll arrange for dinner in my suite and send a car for you.

She gulped. That certainly would be private. Private enough to get her into a whole world of trouble…

7

The driver called to say he was outside and Lina hurried down, hoping she didn't look too overdressed. How did you dress for a private assignation in an ex-lover's hotel room? Especially if he was an international celebrity? She decided on a sleek black dress with a simple necklace of uncut gems, as if she were going out to dinner at a fine restaurant. High heels, too, so he wouldn't tower over her.

The driver made no effort at conversation, and in a few minutes they pulled up in front of one of Paris's most extravagant hotels. She'd stayed there herself a few times when in town with her husband. Now she preferred something more low-key. Amadou had given her his room number, so she passed through the opulent lobby without going near the front desk or giving her name to anyone.

Thank goodness for modern technology.

Her pulse ratcheted up as she took the elevator to the top floor. *You're here to tell him there's nothing between you. To be polite and kind and wish him well, then get on with the rest of your life.* She couldn't have him sending her extravagant bouquets, thinking that something more would happen between them.

He opened the door to his suite as she got off the elevator, so she had to walk toward him, eyes on him and his on her, for the entire length of the hallway. She instantly regretted overdressing. He wore a white T-shirt and dark jeans and his feet were bare, as if she were coming over to watch TV with him back in his one-room garret in Zurich. Not that he'd had a TV. Too prosaic for him.

He didn't say anything at all until he'd stepped aside to usher her in, then closed the door behind her. "I'm so glad you came." He didn't kiss her or try to take her in his arms or any of the things she'd been ready to resist. "It was a good idea to meet privately, away from the prying eyes of the press."

"This hotel is not where I would have pictured you." She looked around at the vast suite with its expansive views toward the Arc de Triomphe and its elaborate furnishings. "You must have changed a lot."

It sounded like censure, and maybe it was. It was somehow disappointing that someone so unmaterialistic as Amadou now chose to live in quasi-imperial splendor.

He shrugged. "When in Rome, *tu sais*? This is what people expect of me. My surroundings mean little to me, so why disappoint them?"

"I suppose I take the same view of mine. You do get used to palatial splendor after a while, don't you?" She giggled, surprising herself. *Uh-oh*. That schoolgirl giddiness had come back. Maybe it would have been better if they had shared a quick peck on the cheek. Not touching him at all worsened the sexual tension between them.

"Champagne?" He indicated a bottle chilling in a silver ice bucket. A comically retro touch considering she could see a full bar with a series of refrigerators. "It's from Altaleone."

"That was sweet of you. I know we brag about our champagne being the finest on earth, but I don't suppose it's really true."

"Any champagne drunk in your presence would be the finest to me." He said it simply without a hint of garish flirtation as he poured them both glasses. Their fingertips brushed as he handed her glass to her, and she could swear she felt a jolt of electricity shoot to her toes.

"Thanks."

"To the future." He raised his glass to her.

"Which is a little scary right now, but I'll embrace it."

"Why scary?" He sipped his champagne.

Damn, why did he have to look so good? His tall, broad frame and even his slim bare feet were doing something strange to her insides.

She sighed. "I'm alone now, for the first time in…forever."

The compassion in his eyes made her wish she could eat her words. The last thing she'd intended was to come here with what sounded like a plea for companionship.

"I envy you your big family. I don't imagine they'll be as distant as you expect."

"I know. I suppose that adapting to change

isn't my strong point. But you surprised me when you said you envied me. I thought you said you didn't want children."

"I didn't." He surveyed her over his glass.

"You didn't say or you didn't want them?"

"Both, I guess." His mouth hitched in a smile. "But there are times when I wonder what my life would have been like if I had been crazy enough to start a family."

"It's not too late. You could do like most male celebrities and marry a woman half your age." She congratulated herself on sounding like she cared little about whom he slept with.

He laughed. "No, thanks."

"Why not?"

"Why would I? I prefer a mature woman with years of wisdom to share with me." His dark gaze drifted over her face, and she could swear she felt heat from it travel across the room.

Flatterer. Shame it was working so well. She teetered in her high heels on the thick carpet.

"Come, sit down." He gestured to the elegant sofa. "The kitchen will send dinner as soon as we're ready."

She walked to the sofa as steadily as she could manage, then sat down, arranging her dress primly about her knees. She'd have to go slow with the champagne. She already felt tipsy in Amadou's heady presence.

He came and sat next to her, and the weight of his big body tilted her slightly toward him. She braced herself, trying to think of something light and pointless to say.

"I loved you, you know."

His deep voiced words shocked her so hard she almost spilled her champagne. "What?"

"You heard me." His eyes narrowed just enough to convey how seriously he spoke.

"I didn't know. Honestly." It felt right to say the truth.

"Would it have made a difference?"

He champagne glass sweated in her hand. Would it? *Yes.* No. Would she have defied her family and turned down a prestigious royal marriage for an uncertain future with him?

Amadou sighed. "I suppose you'd have married him anyway. You always were the kind of nice girl who does what people expect of her."

"Not really." She'd had the affair with him, after all. Her prudish and judgmental sister, Liesel, would have died if she'd known. Liesel would die right now if she knew she was here with him in his hotel room. "Though I can't say I've ever been a rebel."

His wistful look turned to a wry smile. "It's not too late to start."

"What am I supposed to rebel from?"

"Quiet boredom. Settling for less than you deserve."

"I'm quite sure I don't deserve to live in a magnificent three-hundred-year-old palace, but I certainly can't complain about it. And why would you think I'm bored? I have plenty to do."

"Tending your roses?" His brow lifted slightly.

55

"Something like that. Just because you wouldn't enjoy it doesn't mean that I don't. You didn't want children, and I devoted my life to raising mine and enjoyed every minute of it. So, you see, we weren't meant for each other at all."

She said it boldly, feeling it with conviction.

He watched her for a moment, his brow slightly furrowed with concentration. "Maybe with you, my life would have been different."

"Why did you never have children?" It was the kind of socially unacceptable question you knew to never ask anyone. But since he was apparently accusing her of ruining his life—or something—it felt appropriate.

His chest rose slightly, inside his white T-shirt. "I was afraid."

"Of what?" She wasn't going to let him off with the kind of empty answer that went over well in magazine interviews.

He drew in a deep breath. "My father...he was a bad man."

"I thought you never knew him." She couldn't fully remember the story he'd told her. It had been short on details even back then.

"I didn't, but I knew enough to be...afraid. Of what I might pass on to my children."

"What do you mean, *bad*?" In the nature versus nurture debate she knew from firsthand experience that nature was a big deal, but could the wrong DNA curse someone from birth? She didn't believe that.

"He arranged for my mother to come here from Mali with the promise of work in a hotel." He frowned. "He kept her locked up here in

Paris, forcing her to work in an illegal sweatshop to pay her debt, which kept growing."

"Modern-day slavery," she said slowly.

He nodded. "One night he took my mother by force." He pushed his words out through almost closed lips.

"Oh, no." The words rushed out. "I'm so sorry. Goodness. I can see that would be hard—" She had no idea what to say. No wonder he hadn't told her. No one wanted to be the product of a rape.

"It's okay. She escaped from him that night and never saw him again. My history is just part of who I am."

"Have you always known?"

"Since I was about eleven. I kept pressing my mom, pushing her, begging her to tell me who my father was and getting angry when she wouldn't. She finally admitted it, and then I hated myself for forcing the issue."

"You never told me."

"I never told anyone. Not until years later. It was still an open wound when I was with you."

She sighed and sipped her champagne. "I suppose what doesn't kill you makes you stronger."

"And sometimes the pain leaves you in the form of beautiful music." A smile lit his eyes again, even though the rest of his face still looked serious. "I probably wouldn't be who I am if my dad was a nice accountant or engineer and I'd had a pampered existence."

"And the world would have missed out on your talent." Phew. Negative into a positive.

Next time she got the urge to ask a probing question, she was going to keep her trap shut.

His smile shone quietly in his eyes for a moment. Then he tilted his head. "Perhaps I should call for dinner. Would you like the salmon? It's pretty decent."

"That sounds lovely." He called in their order, and they went back to polite chatter. What a relief.

"More champagne?"

"Why not?"

The delicate poached salmon and braised vegetables were delicious—as you'd expect at such an expensive hotel—and they managed to keep the conversation on conventional topics like what all her children were doing. She could talk about them all day, and with all their accomplishments it was easy to do. "Did you know my son Darias is a world-renowned artist? He's hoping to keep painting even now that he's king. He's set up a studio in the top of the medieval castle in the town center where he and his wife, Emma, live."

She didn't mention how his wife was a former gallery assistant whom he'd paid to pretend to be his wife for a year. They'd made such a lovely couple at the lavish royal wedding that neither she nor anyone else had guessed it was all an act. Life was always more complicated than it seemed on the surface.

"I've seen his work. He has a true appreciation for the beauty of women—both inside and outside. I'm sure he gets that from being raised by such a fine woman himself."

She laughed. "Flattery doesn't work on me at all. Royals hear so much of it that we grow to hate it."

Amadou laughed loudly, probably grateful for some honesty after all the pleasant chatter. "I'll do my best to be brutally frank." He sat back in his chair and looked steadily at her face for a moment. "Did you miss me at all?"

"Of course I did." She spoke the truth. "You were my closest friend, and under the circumstances I could hardly call you up for a chat."

"I'd have given you all kinds of bad advice." His wolfish smile did something strange to her insides. "Especially late at night when I was missing you in my bed."

"I know." She turned the stem of her wineglass. "And I might well have listened. So I didn't call."

"I ached for you, and there you were in the cheap newspapers, beaming with joy under your tiara." He let out an exhale. "I've never been so jealous in my life as I was of your husband. I'd have liked to challenge him to a duel over you."

She giggled at the idea. "You'd have won."

"Tell me about it." He tilted his head and lowered his thick lashes, regarding her through hooded eyes that gleamed with…something. "And I'd still like to win the prize."

8

Amadou watched Lina's eyes widen. Some would accuse him of being too bold, but if anything he'd showed restraint.

There was no "might" in his mind. He intended to claim her, if only for one night. "Would you like to hear the new song I just wrote?"

"I'd love that." The relief in her eyes showed that she was glad of a change of subject. He wanted to laugh. Didn't she realize his song would be about her?

"I wrote it last night and laid down some tracks in the studio this morning with my band." He pulled up the MP3 on his phone. Just the background beat and the guitar.

He stood, feeling suddenly shy. He'd written plenty of songs about Lina over the years but never performed one to her face—at least not since they were both kids.

He turned and walked into the middle of the sitting room, as the music poured out of his portable speakers and flowed around them.

Lina looked so beautiful sitting there, her blonde hair falling softly to her shoulders, her blue eyes bright with anticipation and her cheeks flushed from champagne.

Damn but he longed to take her in his arms right now.

He let the tension build, filling his creative well, growing the song inside him. Finally, when he couldn't stand it anymore, he let the words spill out.

Lina had moved to the sofa, glad to stretch out and relax. Making conversation had made her tense. Watching his mouth move made her want to kiss him. His gestures made her wish he would touch her. And also that he wouldn't, because where would that lead?

She relished the opportunity to sit back and listen to him sing. It would give her a chance to think up a polite excuse to leave. An early-morning hair appointment, perhaps? Might as well choose something that made her seem dull and shallow.

Amadou didn't use a mic. He hung his head for a moment, moving slightly to the beat as the opening bars of the music played, then suddenly he threw his head back and started to sing.

In the relatively small space of the hotel suite, his voice rang with raw power that emanated from every muscle of his body. Hoping to relax, instead she found herself sitting to attention, rapt, hanging on every note that echoed off the elaborate plaster moldings of the high ceiling.

Then she noticed the lyrics.
She was always there inside me
Hidden in my mind

So many years apart meant nothing...

He stared right at her, his gaze trapping hers, his words penetrating her brain.

I don't think she knew it

But I was there inside her all the time

She swallowed. Was he right? Had she been carrying Amadou—or feelings for him—all through her marriage to Emil?

Yes.

Impossible, though. She didn't think about him. Not much, anyway. But she couldn't deny there was still something powerful between them. Probably just that chemistry people made so much of. It worked like an expensive perfume, creating a connection between people even when there was no real reason for them to communicate.

He kept singing, and she deliberately tried not to listen to the lyrics. His strong voice was transfixing enough already. And his eyes, the way they stared at her, as if they could see right through to her thoughts.

Suddenly he stopped, and she realized she'd been holding her breath. She drew in air and managed to conjure a smile. "That was wonderful."

He cocked his head, challenging her. "Wonderful?"

He thought her comment sounded phony. Which it was. *Wonderful* was a word you'd use to praise an elaborate floral arrangement, a beautiful bridal gown, or perhaps a pleasant tea party for a few hundred of your favorite foreign diplomats.

62

"Powerful," she attempted. "Moving."

"Thank you." Now one corner of his lip lifted into a wry smile. "I'd hate to think I hadn't moved you."

"You move audiences of a thousand people," she said, trying to make it seem like it wasn't just her.

"A thousand? I played to ninety thousand in the Wembley Arena last month."

"Really? I didn't know anywhere could hold that many people."

"I bet there are a lot of things you don't know." He walked toward her.

"No doubt." She pushed another smile to her lips. "I never claimed to be perfect."

He sat down on the sofa next to her, which sent a shockwave of awareness through her.

She should have sat on the chair instead.

"You don't have to claim to be perfect." He took her hand. *Uh-oh.* And kissed it. *Double uh-oh.* Heat flashed through her, up her arm and to her face. "It's enough for you to be simply—you."

Before she could respond—or even gather her thoughts—his lips met hers in a fiery explosion of...whatever that was that happened between them when they got too close.

This time the kiss deepened instantly. Her hands flew to his neck, drawing him to her. He wrapped his around her, enveloping her in his warmth.

I've missed you so much.

A line from his song and from her own heart pulsed in her head. She'd forgotten what it was like to experience this kind of passion. To have her whole body come alive in a man's arms.

Her fingers wove into his hair, feeling the familiar shape of his head, then down his back, where they plucked at his T-shirt, groping for the hot skin beneath it.

His lips made a trail of kisses across her cheekbone and to her neck, where he hit an erogenous zone and made her gasp. His hands roamed over her, exploring her back and touching the sides of her breasts, which made her shiver with pleasure.

I've missed you so much.

Why did she leave him? It seemed insane. So long ago she couldn't even conjure her actual reasoning at the time, just her much-repeated official version of it.

Her fingers probed under his T-shirt and pressed into the hard muscle of his back. She felt his belly contract as he sucked in a breath.

"In thirty years my feelings for you haven't changed one bit." He breathed the words into her neck, and she felt the truth of them in her heart.

Mine neither. She had the presence of mind not to speak her thoughts. Still, she couldn't seem to stop her hands from wandering lower, to caress his hard backside and powerful thighs.

She'd forgotten what it felt like to be with such a strong man. Her late husband, Emil, was…an intellectual—not given to exercise or physical development. Amadou was naturally built like an athlete. He approached his daily life with such muscular energy that every day was a full-body workout. If anything his body looked better than ever—fuller and more substantial but still lean as a college student.

The effect on her own body was electrifying. Her insides quaked and yearned for him. And when she felt his fingers on the zipper of her dress, the only thought she could summon was *yes!*

He lowered the zipper carefully, sliding his fingers over the bare skin of her back. She shivered in anticipation of feeling his skin against hers. As soon as he reached the bottom she tugged at the hem of his T-shirt and together they pulled it over his head.

"Stand up." His whispered command brought her to her feet, and she realized he was about to release her dress at the shoulders and let it drop to the floor. Sudden panic surged through her. He'd last seen her naked when she was a skinny girl of twenty without a single stretch mark.

What if he saw her body and was repulsed, or at least unpleasantly surprised?

As if sensing her hesitation, he held her close and kissed her until she started to relax again. Then, releasing her only far enough from him that there was room for her dress to slide down, he eased it off her shoulders and over her arms.

As it fell to the floor he let out a ragged sigh and ran his hands over her sides.

"I never thought I'd hold you in my arms again," he murmured. He cupped her backside, then slid his arms around her waist and pressed her naked body against him. Her insides shimmied. "This is a dream come true."

Emotion welled inside Lina. She hadn't dreamed about meeting Amadou again. If anything she'd dreaded it, maybe because she knew there was still buried emotion deep inside her. Unfulfilled longing that had lain dormant somewhere in her heart throughout her long marriage, just waiting for the right conditions to burst forth and bloom again.

She shouldn't be doing this.

Her nipples grew tight against his hard chest. He made her feel young inside. Her heart beat like a drum, and her breathing grew unsteady. Passion snuck over her and made her skin hot and her thoughts confused.

She wasn't supposed to get this overexcited at her age.

It didn't feel...safe.

Still, her fingers wandered to the button on his pants and undid it. Then she unzipped them, and together they slid his pants and underwear down over his strong thighs until he stepped out of them.

The sight of Amadou naked always had an alarming effect on her, and nothing had changed. Her insides clamored when she saw his proud erection, and she ached to have him buried deep in her.

Again.

As they kissed and caressed, reveling in each others' bodies, there was an eerie familiarity that made the strange situation seem somehow totally natural.

"I want to make love to you," he whispered softly in her ear. "May I?"

Her heart squeezed. "Yes." He'd asked her like that the first time all those years ago. The thoughtful gesture had surprised her since everything else about him was so bold. She'd given the same answer then.

He led her into his bedroom, where he retrieved a condom from a drawer and rolled it on deftly. Her anxious self-consciousness had vanished. His appreciation of her body—of her—was so evident and obvious she almost wanted to laugh.

He lifted her onto the bed and her skin tingled with awareness as he climbed over her and kissed her softly on the lips. She held her breath as he entered her, but her body welcomed him, drawing him deep, and soon she relaxed and they started to move together.

Oh, my.

Sensations she hadn't experienced in decades rippled through her. He moved with the same confidence, the same tender affection that had stirred her when she was too young and shallow to realize how much it meant.

Now she'd lived long enough to know that this kind of passion was rare. That the emotions flooding her right now were feelings you could go through an entire lifetime and never know.

She inhaled his scent—intoxicating as always—and drew it down into her core. As they kissed she felt herself growing drunk on the taste of him. He moved them both with such ease, guiding the rhythm and moving them between positions in a way that felt both completely natural and utterly exciting. Being with him felt effortless, inevitable, like the sunset and the sunrise, or getting caught in the rain of a sudden storm.

When her climax finally overtook her she cried out, then immediately apologized. Surely decades of royal training should have disciplined such an outburst out of her? A palace or a hotel had far too many employees who could overhear a moment of passionate indiscretion.

"Don't apologize," he murmured, still panting hard after his own release. "That's the most exciting sound I've heard in years. And as a musician I am something of an expert."

They both laughed, their chests shaking against each other. Then he pulled his arms around her again and held her so tight she could hardly breathe.

"Now that I have you in my arms I don't want to let you go again."

She giggled against his chest. "I'm not sure I want to go anywhere." She felt so relaxed after their lovemaking.

"If I let you go you might walk away and go marry some prince and I won't see you again for thirty years."

"I won't marry again," she said quite honestly. "It was a good marriage but once was enough."

"Yes, you will." He said it with slow deliberation. "You won't be able to help yourself. You're traditional at your core. I can't imagine you having a relationship that wasn't leading to marriage."

"I did it before. With you."

"Yes, and then you waltzed off and married someone else."

"This time I definitely will not be doing that."

"Because you're staying with me?"

She bit her lip. Could she stay overnight? She hadn't brought a change of clothes or any makeup other than lipstick. Still, the thought of leaving made her heart contract painfully. "Perhaps for tonight."

He kissed her forehead softly. "That's good enough for me. If I can hold you in my arms for one entire night, I could probably die happy."

"Don't say that!" Her words came out with more force than she intended.

He squeezed her. "I'm so sorry. I didn't mean it like that. I almost forgot that you recently lost your husband."

Ouch. The elephant in the room shifted. Emil was now right here in the bedroom with them— in their thoughts. Even though you couldn't technically cheat on a dead man, she couldn't help feeling that she'd betrayed him in some way.

"It's still a bit raw, that's all." She inhaled as much as she could with Amadou's chest pressed over hers. With him still inside her... "It was very sudden. Unexpected."

Tears welled inside her. What was she doing? She hadn't been a widow for even one full year yet, and already she was naked in the arms of another man? And having surprising and disconcerting feelings for him. It was all too much, too soon.

69

"I have to go."

9

Amadou's driver took Lina back to her hotel—in their lifestyle there was always someone who knew your most intimate movements. She was a little surprised at how easily Amadou let her go. She had promised to see him again before she left Paris, and to be honest she was already looking forward to it.

You're mad!

Her conscience upbraided her for giving in to foolish desire. But some other, more reckless part of her was thrilled that she still possessed the ability to desire after all these years.

She barely slept that night and woke in a state of semi-bliss, her body still reveling in the pleasure she'd experienced last night. Would it have been wonderful or terrifying to wake in his arms?

Terrifying probably. This reunion affair wasn't going anywhere. Sooner or later she'd be licking her wounds, and deservedly so, considering how she'd treated him when they were younger.

Her phone's ringtone made her jump. Was it him?

No. And the name that popped up on the screen made her heart sink. Her sanctimonious sister, Liesel—who had skipped over marriage and family to devote herself full time to criticizing others. "Good morning."

"I heard you were in Paris."

Luckily, Liesel lived in Germany.

"Yes, visiting Callista."

"I just arrived here myself to do a little shopping."

Lina's gut clenched. "You're in Paris?" Of course Liesel knew nothing about Amadou, either now or years ago, but her beady pale eyes rarely missed a trick. "Where are you staying?" Far away, hopefully.

"Prince de Galles."

Lina swallowed. Amadou's hotel. "Oh."

"I had to battle my way through a crowd of reporters when I got out of my taxi this morning. Some African musician is here, and he just got nominated for an award. I mean, really! The place is mobbed when one chooses the Prince de Galles for peace and privacy."

Was she talking about Amadou? *He's French, not African.* She managed to hold her tongue, wondering what the award could be. She paid no attention to the music scene.

"But in the event that I manage to fight my way out again, I was thinking we could meet for lunch at Siri's."

Lina racked her brain for a reason to refuse. And failed. Being royal meant that you couldn't make enemies of anyone, least of all family. "I could do that. Is one okay?" That should give her time to recover and maybe get her hair done to revive her facade of respectability before meeting Liesel.

"Let's make it noon."

"Okay." Liesel always liked to be difficult. "See you then." Hopefully she could escape fast. She hung up and wondered if—and how—she could warn Amadou about the potential enemy in his camp, but then he'd never even heard of her sister and would hardly see her as a threat to himself so that would just be weird.

She Googled his name and "award" and found he was up for a Grammy. Then she texted him to congratulate him. She was just being polite. Really! It was the kind of thing anyone would do.

Thanks. I want to take you for lunch.

She sighed. And spent a hilarious second wondering what would happen if she invited him to join her and Liesel. Liesel would be polite to his face, most likely, at least. Like her she'd been expensively trained at the finest schools, but afterward she'd berate her for dating someone outside her social circle and destroying the family's reputation.

Never mind that Amadou was richer and more famous than any of them. Certainly more well-loved.

I can't. My awful sister is in town. And she's at your hotel.

Her phone rang. It was him. "How awful is she?" His deep, melodious voice stirred her insides.

"Unbelievably awful. You have no idea."

"But you can't cancel on her because it's your family duty to meet her for lunch."

"Exactly." She laughed. "You know me too well."

"I could trip her in the lobby."

"Don't. She'd sue you."

"How about dinner, then?"

Lina bit her lip as a warm flush of sensation rose through her. She would love to have dinner with him again. "I'm nervous that we're going to be noticed." She could hardly go to his hotel now that her sister was staying there. And if they ate in a restaurant, anyone could see them.

"Would that be so bad?"

"Yes. I hate being gossiped about. I'm still officially in mourning. It would look bad if I was—"

"Out on the town with a hot, young Grammy nominee."

"You're not younger than me! You're a year older. But yes. And there are my children to think of. I need to keep a low profile."

"I understand." He spoke slowly, and she could almost hear wheels turning in his brain. "I know of a quiet place just outside the city. No people to recognize you. Total privacy. I'll pick you up at seven. I'll call your room and you can come right out to the car. Secrecy in all things."

"Uh…" warring factions in her brain staged a mock battle. It didn't last long. "Okay. See you then."

As soon as she'd hung up she realized she'd planned an entire day without consulting Callista, who she was purportedly there to visit.

Still, her body tingled with rash excitement at the prospect of seeing Amadou again.

As long as no one knew about their crazy reunion romance, her eventual pain at being ditched by him would be private and she would handle it the way she'd handled all the trauma and upheaval of the past year. As long as no one found out about them she'd be fine.

"Oh, my goodness." Liesel flounced into the chic café and slammed her bag down on the table. "The problem with Paris is that it's full of bloody French people."

"It's known for that." Lina sipped her coffee. It was utterly pointless trying to school Liesel on any subject. Her mind had been closed for decades.

"Shame they have the most beautiful leatherwork. I'm forced to come here whenever I need new boots."

"Custom?"

"Of course, darling. I have this little man on Faubourg Saint-Honoré. I don't know what I'd do without him."

Lina wondered where Amadou bought his boots. Did he have them custom-made?

Focus! "Callista is loving her new job. They're on the brink of some big new discovery."

"Riveting. Just make sure she doesn't marry anyone unsuitable. Paris is full of all sorts of unsavory types. And your children are showing a rebellious streak. I still can't believe Darias—the king of Altaleone—married a nobody whom he'd hired as a stand-in bride."

"We all love her. It was very fortuitous. And he only made the arrangement with her because he was under so much pressure to produce a wife. I hope that the rest of my children can follow their heart and take the time to find someone they truly love."

"Nonsense. Aunt Friedl masterminded your marriage to Emil and look how well that turned out."

"True." She forced a smile. True, they'd enjoyed a comfortable life and raised ten wonderful children, but since running into Amadou again she had a distinct sense that she'd missed out on something else.

Passion.

"It's your job as their mother to strategize, plan and execute their future unions in order to avoid disaster." Liesel waved rudely at a waiter and ordered two coffees in terrible French. "It's simply your royal duty."

"Uh, I hate to point this out…" Lina found herself feeling reckless. "But you've never married."

Liesel sniffed the air. "I never found anyone adequate. Far better to remain single than to lower oneself."

Lina sighed. "Don't you get lonely?"

"Not at all. I find men rather tiresome even in small doses. Really—who doesn't? I suppose this is why women encourage them to shoot and play golf and other time-consuming pursuits."

Lina laughed. "I suspect my daughters will be marrying men with demanding careers, not nineteenth-century aristocrats with time on their hands. But I have no intention of interfering in any way."

"What if they all decide to marry Americans?" Liesel lifted a penciled brow. "Or worse?"

"I will welcome whoever they choose. And for the record I'd be delighted for any of them to choose to have a partner of the same gender."

"My goodness." Liesel looked appropriately scandalized. "What would Emil say?"

Now that Lina had a better idea of what Emil got up to in his spare time—with the kinky Cross of Blood society—she didn't think much would have shocked him. Or that he'd have a right to show any kind of disapproval. "Sometimes people can surprise you."

They ordered lunch and had a dull but harmless conversation about summer hats. All the while Lina's mind kept straying to Amadou and their plans for that night. She wouldn't be able to go back to his hotel this whole trip, not with Liesel staying right there in the same building. She'd never hear the end of it if her sister got wind of her affair. Or even found out that she'd been rash enough to have sex outside of a carefully arranged marriage.

"You do seem distracted today," probed Liesel, snapping a crab leg with manicured fingertips. "Are you getting enough sleep?"

"Of course," she answered, too quickly. She didn't want her sister to know that she'd tossed and turned last night, thinking of her lover. "I'm just out of my element here in Paris. There's so much to do and so little time."

"Indeed. When are you leaving?"

She hesitated. "I'm not sure yet. I…I…it will depend on Callista's schedule." She didn't want to state a definite plan, then find herself needing to backtrack. "There's some big party next week she wants me to attend."

"Callista doesn't strike me as a party girl."

"It's just one of those things that everyone is going to. A charity fundraiser. I accepted my invitation months ago. If I'm back in Altaleone I'll just send regrets. I don't like those big dos, but if I'm here anyway I suppose I'll go."

"You really should be back home, making sure Darias fully understands his royal duties."

"Darias is fine." Lina lifted a brow. "You don't need to concern yourself with the management of Altaleone."

"Of course not, darling. I'm just concerned about you."

"I'm also fine."

"It's just that you look a little…flushed." Liesel's eyes narrowed.

Lina felt her skin heat. She might well look flushed after the excitement of last night. Every cell of her body had come alive in Amadou's arms. "I'm fine." She toyed with her quiche. "Just a lot on my mind."

"It's never easy getting another year older at our age," simpered Liesel. "I need to find you a gift, don't I?"

"Nonsense. I don't know why everyone feels the need to buy me something for my birthday. I can buy whatever I want."

"Don't rub it in, dear. I'm not impoverished myself."

"I wasn't trying to say..." Never mind. Whatever you said to Liesel was the wrong thing. "I need to do some shopping this afternoon." She wanted to buy something new to wear tonight. Something elegant and tasteful, but possibly a bit less...royal than her usual attire.

"Fine. I'll come with you. It's important to have someone honest with you once you're past a certain age."

Great. Lina's heart sank. "I think I'm just going to hit Galleries Lafayette and Printemps. Nowhere too fancy."

"Ugh, there are so many people there."

"I like people," she said brightly.

"You're on your own then. I'm going to my equestrian tailor. Let me call him and have him fit me in. I believe I've lost an inch off my waist since I gave up carbohydrates." She pulled out her phone, and Lina heaved a sigh of relief as Liesel browbeat him into rearranging his afternoon for her.

I'm looking forward to tonight.

The sound of the text made her jump, and Amadou's name on the text made her startle. She really should put something more cryptic in her phone's address book, so anyone peeking would think a florist or caterer was calling.

She wanted to reply, just to be polite, but she didn't want to encourage him too much with Liesel still sitting here.

Me too. She typed it quickly, then tucked her

phone into her bag.

"What was that?"

"Oh, nothing." How guilty did that sound?

And she'd be guilty of even more after tonight.

10

Amadou felt as nervous as a boy on his first date when he pulled up to Lina's hotel. Usually he maintained an easy-come, easy-go attitude to relationships—which went nicely with his nomadic existence—but the way he felt tonight you'd think he was planning to propose or something.

He wasn't.

But he did have another plan that rather surprised him and would probably surprise her, too

He texted her that he was outside. It felt rude not to go in to get her, but he knew how privacy conscious she was and the press was extra interested in his movements with the surprise Grammy nomination for his latest release. He'd concentrated on touring and hadn't been nominated for one in years. Some people probably thought he was dead.

He laughed.

Normally this was when his driver and confidant would turn to him and ask what was so funny. But he'd given him the night off, to assure total confidentiality for Lina.

She didn't respond to his text and he was beginning to wonder if maybe she'd got cold feet when suddenly the porter opened the doors and a glow emerged, sheltered from the light drizzle by a large hotel umbrella. The glow, of course, was Lina, her hair arranged in an updo and a pale raincoat drawn about her.

He felt a smile spreading across his face. She really did shine like a light wherever she went. It wasn't just her outer beauty, it came from within, from her warm personality and the love she shared so readily with others.

He leaped out to open the door for her, hoping that no one would recognize him in the dark and the rain.

Her shy smile stirred his heart. "Good evening," he said softly, not wanting to draw the porter's suspicion.

"Good evening to you, too."

He wanted to kiss her but restrained himself. There'd be time for that later.

She congratulated him again on his Grammy nomination, and they talked for a while about the ups and downs of his career and how gratifying it was to keep finding fresh audiences for his unusual music.

Then she frowned. "Where are we going?"

She'd noticed that they were leaving central Paris and heading out to the suburbs.

He braced himself slightly. "My mother's house."

He turned to catch her wide-eyed stare. "Oh."

"I wanted to find somewhere away from all

the cameras. And your supposedly terrible sister. And my mom is a fan of yours. She reads those silly royal magazines."

"Does she know that we...know each other?"

"Of course." He smiled cryptically. He hadn't told her anything other than that they were old friends, but she wasn't born yesterday.

"Well, I can't wait to meet her." Lina's diplomatic response, delivered with a warm smile, was no less than he'd expect of her. "I really should bring her a gift. Can we stop for some flowers?"

He laughed. "At this time of night? Don't worry. She won't be expecting anything. And she has a cook so we're not causing her any work."

"Tell me about her. What does she do? Is she retired?" Lina's own parents were long dead, since they'd both been almost middle aged when they had her.

"She was a schoolteacher for nearly twenty years, teaching French to immigrant children in the suburbs, but now she's retired and spends most of her time in her garden."

"We have something in common, then. I love my garden. It's a shame it will be too dark to see hers."

The drive was filled with relaxing conversation and reassuring glances, and he arrived at his mom's gates with a sense of heightened anticipation. He didn't start to get really nervous until the gates opened, and they pulled up the long gravel driveway.

Would his mom assume he was bringing Lina to visit because he intended to propose to her? Would she think such an aspiration—marrying a royal—outlandish and arrogant? Would she welcome Lina or would she be—as sometimes happened—suspicious and prickly with his guest?

Somehow everything mattered far more than it should.

Lina managed to clamber out of the car before Amadou could rush around to help her. "I'm fine, really. People act like I'm helpless, but I'm not. I should open your door for you. Did you know I have a fitness trainer three times a week back in Altaleone?"

"I'm not at all surprised." His eyes roamed daringly up and down her body, making her feel like he could see right through her thin raincoat and the brand-new silky top and skirt beneath.

She would have worn something quite different if she had known she was meeting his mother. His mother! It was hard to even remember that someone like Amadou—a kind of living rock god—had been born to a human mother. Which was silly because he'd mentioned her before. Still, she didn't ever really think she'd get to meet her.

That seemed so…serious.

The front door of the large house opened, an archway of light in the rain-damp darkness, and a small female form appeared in silhouette.

"Hello, Mama. I want you to meet Carolina. She's one of my oldest and dearest friends."

Lina found his words—hey, she'd been friend-zoned—both reassuring and a little depressing. She climbed the steps and extended her hand, which was embraced in his mother's two soft palms. The older woman's dark eyes met hers, and she could feel them boring into her, asking questions. All kinds of questions.

"It's so nice to meet you…" What should she call her?

"Please call me Aurelie."

"Please call me Lina." She smiled her warmest, professional smile. *Amadou's told me so much about you. Have you lived here long? My, what weather we're having!* All her usual lines seemed embarrassing and inappropriate under the circumstances.

"Do come inside." Amadou's mother moved slowly. She must be in her seventies, a delicately built woman, very elegant in a black sweater and patterned cigarette pants, her silver hair cut quite short. She led them into a beautiful, dimly lit living room. "You're not the first royal person to visit this house." She turned with a shy smile. "Marie Antoinette used it as a summer house from time to time."

"It's gorgeous. Amadou tells me you have a lovely garden…" The conversation went smoothly and easily. For some reason she'd pictured his mother being some painfully shy immigrant with barely any English. Maybe she had been once, but that was a long time ago. They talked about places they liked to visit, Amadou's alternately endearing and infuriating nomadic tendencies and—at last—his mother lamented about his refusal to create a family.

"I would have loved him to give me grandchildren." She shot him a scolding look.

"I bought you Napoleon." He glanced at the sweet black-and-white dog curled up on the sofa next to her.

She tutted. "And he is my heart, but it's hardly the same thing." She sighed. "You have children, don't you?"

"Ten of them. Only five pregnancies, though. Twins run in my husband's family."

Aurelie looked shocked. "I would never have guessed."

This was where Lina often thought she should admit to the tummy tuck she'd been talked into ten years ago, as well as the personal trainer, but as usually she just shrugged and smiled.

"I would have loved to have more children, but it wasn't meant to be," Aurelie added.

"Amadou could still marry a young woman and give you grandchildren." Lina said the words through gritted teeth.

Aurelie laughed and looked lovingly at her son. "Unfortunately he's far too sensible for that."

Now Amadou laughed. "Are we ever going to eat? This conversation is embarrassing me."

Dinner was as stylish as her host and their surroundings, catered by two adorable young aspiring actors who couldn't help joining in their conversation and gushing over Amadou's Grammy nomination. After dinner they shared strong, rather bitter coffee and handmade chocolates, then his mom excused herself, saying that she needed to get her beauty sleep but that they should stay as long as they wanted.

The caterers had packed up and left, little Napoleon tottered off after his owner, and suddenly they were all alone in the quiet living room.

Lina didn't realize until that moment just how much tension—sexual and otherwise—had built up in her during the hours of proximity and polite conversation.

Amadou's mouth crushed over hers with urgency that showed he felt the same. Relief flooded her veins at the sensation of his arms around her. She kissed him back with uninhibited passion. It was amazing to feel so much for this man and to express it.

They must have kissed for several mindless minutes before she remembered their surroundings. "What would your mom think?"

He shrugged. "I have no idea."

"She's amazing."

"She is. I'm glad you got a chance to meet her." He looked pleased at her praise.

"You never told me she was a teacher." He'd told her she was a maid or cleaner or something like that.

"She wasn't, back when we first knew each other. That came later. After I started making money I pushed her to try out some evening classes and she took it from there." He cocked his head. "She's living proof that you can reinvent yourself in midlife and go on to have a full career doing something different."

Lina exhaled slowly. "I'm not sure I'm up for a new career. Have I ever really had one? I'm not sure that royal wife actually counts."

He laughed, a truly amused giggle. "I'm sure you were a lot more than that. Diplomat, hostess and of course a mother. I bet no one ever believes you had ten children." He gave a steamy glance down at her body. "What's your secret?"

It was her turn to shrug and smile mysteriously. "It wouldn't be a secret if I told you, would it?"

He stared at her for a moment, let his gaze drift to her lips, then kissed her again. It felt okay to have secrets with Amadou. Everyone had them. Her husband certainly had. No one ever knew everything about anybody.

Her belly shimmered as his fingertips grazed it through her thin top. She let her hands stray to his biceps. So hard and powerful. Everything about Amadou was intense, strong, a little overwhelming.

She gasped slightly as his hand slid inside her blouse and his thumb grazed her nipple. The intimate touch sent a jolt of arousal through her like he'd hit a switch. Her blood heated and she leaned toward him, closing her eyes and inhaling his masculine scent.

"I want to make love to you." He breathed the words into her neck, hot and insistent.

"Here?"

"Now." He was already removing her top. Were they really going to make love on his mom's expensively upholstered sofa? She felt like a teenager again—except that as a teenager she'd probably have been more sensible.

Sensible had deserted her. They tugged their clothes off and eagerly pressed skin to skin. Then Amadou sucked her nipples to hard peaks. She feathered kisses over the hard muscle of his chest, and down to his rock-hard erection.

Then she stopped.

11

Lina hesitated. Her husband had told her that giving a man pleasure this way was undignified. Something expected of a whore, not a wife.

Of course this was the man who had brief, vanilla sex with her, then apparently satisfied his less conventional urges with an ancient sex society devoted to keeping royal proclivities—and infidelities—under a cloak of secrecy.

Amadou's erection shifted slightly, as if anticipating the touch of her lips. She decided to indulge her desires, first licking the tip, then taking it into her mouth and sucking eagerly.

His tortured groans only fueled her own inner fires. She wanted to go on sucking him, but the desire to feel him inside her grew more intense until she rose up and pressed herself against him. "I want you."

His only reply was a ragged breath, half buried in a kiss, as he lowered her to the soft cushions of the sofa, sheathed himself with a condom and entered her with exquisite care. The sensations were so powerful she climaxed almost immediately, but—her insides still pulsing around him—she wanted more.

As he moved inside her, deeper and deeper, she knew she wanted to climb on top of him. Again, this was something she hadn't done since she'd last been with Amadou. Her husband had always treated her with the respect and dignity due to his royal bride, and royal brides apparently did not ride cowgirl.

But she hadn't forgotten. Amadou helped her ease herself into position, and it all came back as if she'd last made love to him yesterday. This time, though, she appreciated the intimacy and tenderness of his touch.

When he whispered her name it excited her as it had always done, but somehow being older and wiser made everything more powerful, more meaningful. Back then she hadn't known how perfect their partnership was. She hadn't known that she'd never feel anything quite like it again. That compared with Amadou any other man would be a disappointment and a let down.

Traitorous thoughts, to be sure. And ones she'd never let herself entertain while her husband was alive. Or even afterward, in her grief at losing her best friend and the father of her children. But he'd never made love to her like this.

Never let her make love *to him* like this.

She rode Amadou slowly, then faster, guiding them both to an explosive climax that flung her forward onto him and left them both gasping and perspiring into the designer fabric of his mom's sofa.

When she stopped gasping, she suddenly wondered. "Did I make too much noise?"

He laughed. "I have no idea. My mom is a sound sleeper, though."

"And probably far too discreet to listen. Still, let's get dressed. I can't sit and talk to you naked in your mom's living room."

Chuckling like teenagers who've just gotten away with something, they tugged their clothes back on, then wrapped themselves into an embrace on the sofa again.

"You do realize this isn't normal?" Amadou spoke softly into her hair.

"Two full-grown adults acting like naughty teenagers?"

"No." He pulled back enough to look into her eyes. "Two full-grown adults with such a deep and powerful connection."

She swallowed. There was something— different—between them. Love? No. Love was the feeling that grew inside you along with loyalty and duty to the people you cared about. In many ways this was the opposite of that as it threatened to tug her from her duty and from the people who needed her.

Lust. Passion.

"Just one of those things, I guess." She tried to say it lightly, to shrug off the deep feelings that rose inside her when she was around Amadou.

"I worked really hard to put you out of my mind," he said, expression deadly serious. "It took a long time, and I finally succeeded." His eyes shimmered with emotion. "Or I thought I did. Now all my hard work is ruined."

She couldn't tell if he was joking or being

serious. It was always hard to tell with Amadou.

He tilted his head. "Was it hard for you to forget me? Or did I just slip out of your mind the day you left me?"

She inhaled slowly. She didn't want to hurt him, but she didn't want to lie to him, either. He didn't deserve that. "I suppose that unlike you I saw it coming so I was prepared. I'd been groomed from birth to marry someone suitable and strategic. Seriously, it was the kind of thing my family discussed at Sunday lunch when I was as young as twelve."

"You have got to be joking." He looked suitably appalled.

"Nope." She wished she could laugh about it. "They said that because I was pretty I was the best hope of continuing the family name and fortunes. Liesel was too plain—they said that openly too, right in front of her—so their hopes all rested on me."

"No wonder she's a bit crabby."

"Truly."

"But you just went along with their plan like it actually made sense?"

She blinked. "I wanted to make my parents happy. To make them proud. I knew that my looks were my best asset. I was the pretty one, and Liesel was the smart one. I wasn't going to attend university and have a big career, so my job was to find a good husband and make my family proud."

Amadou stared. "It may have been another century, but it was the twentieth century, not the eighteenth."

"I admit that from where I stand now, it all seems ridiculous. I would no more push my children into a strategic marriage than I would sell them into slavery. It was another era back then, though. Look at poor Princess Diana—married off to a much older man who cheated on her. Things have changed a lot since then. At least I hope they have."

"Maybe you should have told me I was just a temporary fling. Part of your last gasp of freedom." The glint of humor in his eyes warred with the low tone of his voice.

"I thought it was the same for you. I knew I wasn't your first girlfriend. I knew I wouldn't be your last. I guess I didn't think it was that serious." They hadn't lived together—she'd been in an all-girls dorm at her expensive school—or even discussed it. Or anything beyond their plans for the following weekend.

"Maybe I didn't realize how serious it was until it was over." He stroked her cheek. "I suppose I didn't know how deeply I'd fallen in love with you until I tried to fall out of love again."

Lina's breath stuck in her chest. For some reason his words hit her like a blow to the chest. He should hate her after how she'd treated him. "It wasn't easy to leave you. I tried to do it the way you'd rip off a Band-Aid."

"Because I wasn't the kind of lover you could bring home to Mama and Papa."

She didn't know what to say. "They were very snobbish. They definitely wouldn't have approved."

"Of me being a street musician or me being black?"

"Both." She didn't try to prevaricate. "They would have been really upset and told me to leave you immediately."

"So you preemptively avoided the ugly confrontation by doing it before they could meet me."

She nodded, and to her surprise hot tears filled her eyes and flooded her throat. "I should be ashamed. I think I am ashamed. I guess I never really looked at it that way before."

Amadou took her face in his hands. "I didn't mean to make you cry. I'm sorry. You were just trying to be a good girl and make your family happy. Any parent would be proud of you. My mom was probably crying into her pillow in Paris worrying about me—with good reason—so in a lot of ways you're the better person than me."

"You're sweet, but I can see that I was just weak."

He shrugged. "Not everyone is born strong. You became strong, though. Your beautiful family is a testament to that, and you wouldn't have them if you'd run away with me."

She smiled through her tears. "True."

Amadou marveled at his restraint. She shed tears, and he acted like he was a stranger to emotion. He would let his feelings out later in a song.

How did she still look so lovely? And all the

more gorgeous flushed and glowing from making sweet love with him.

He certainly hadn't expected that to happen in his mother's elegant living room. If anything he'd thought they might settle for a discreet kiss in the car. He wasn't trying to rush into anything hot and heavy with Lina.

Partly because he knew it would scare her into hiding. And partly because this experience was taking a toll on him. He'd spent years getting over her, and now he found himself diving back into her embrace like a just-rescued drowning man who hurls himself back into the ocean.

Yet here they were. Where was this going?

Even he wasn't rash enough to ask the question aloud.

She patted her hair. "We should get back to Paris."

"I suppose so." He hated the idea. Left to his own devices he'd like to buy another house like this and keep her locked up in it so she couldn't run away from him again.

"Why are you laughing?" She lifted a brow.

"You'd be disturbed by how much I don't want to take you back."

"I don't really want to go back either, but I know I have to."

"Duty calls." He cocked his head. She'd always choose the call of duty, responsibility and family over him. She'd said as much herself.

"Exactly." She straightened her silk top. "Sometimes duty is the only thing that keeps me sane. In the days immediately following my husband's and mother-in-law's deaths, sometimes I thought I might really lose my mind." She lifted her chin. "Sometimes I still do. How can we not have found the murderer? Every day I fear for my son, the new king. If I didn't have functions to attend and have to keep up a brave facade, I might have gone to pieces by now."

"Are there suspects?"

She exhaled. "Nothing solid. They were in a strange secret society that makes me nervous, but my son thinks that the society exists to protect royals, not kill them. No one ever explains anything to me. I know they're keeping secrets from me to save my feelings. All I know is that the killer is still out there."

She'd stiffened while talking about it, and his fingers itched to massage her now tight shoulders. But that felt wrong when she was talking about her late husband's death.

Did she love him?

She must have, surely. At least enough to conceive and raise all those children with him. And Lina was the type who'd love her husband—really love him—simply out of duty. She was the kind of person arranged marriages were made for.

He rose slowly from the sofa, reluctant to tear himself from their beautiful evening. He couldn't be sure of the next time they'd be together. Or even if there would be a next time.

And that half killed him.

97

12

"So you have concrete proof." Amadou walked along the Champs-Elysées with his longtime friend and ally, Jean-Paul. They avoided using the phone and never used email to discuss anything sensitive. You never knew who was watching—as their target would soon find out.

"We have three incriminating phone conversations recorded and one video from a security camera."

"So none of it's legal."

"Nope, and that's why we need the court of public opinion on our side."

Amadou blew out a breath. "Risky. He could sue us."

"Not if two thousand of the most influential people in France can suddenly see him for the kind of fiend he really is. Then the authorities will be forced to crack down on him properly and it will be out of our hands. We've been after him for years; he's slippery as Teflon. I honestly think this is our best shot."

"If I make this announcement at the Gaia event, my cover will be blown for good."

Jean-Paul shrugged. "Your high profile and integrity are essential to making the evidence compelling and newsworthy."

"I suppose you're right. And there will be a lot of reporters there." Amadou still didn't like it much. It was messy and relied too much on other people. He lowered his voice as they moved past a stationary crowd of tourists taking pictures of each other. "I wish I could refuse, but the stakes are too high. I'll do it."

"Great. I've spoken to the event organizers about your doing a brief talk about your musical inspiration and showing a video of one of your early performances. Only you and I know you have entirely different subject matter in mind. Christine is editing the taped phone conversations and will include a brief testimony from Francie, who we rescued last year."

He nodded. "I don't suppose I'll get to see it beforehand."

"No. Too risky. No one will see it, but I will make sure that there is a different tape—from an old concert of yours—for the rehearsals and that this one is switched at the right moment."

Jean-Paul had recently finagled his way onto the board of the Gaia organization, a high-profile big-wig think tank that hosted spectacular events to raise money for charity. In recent years their parties were so high profile that it was considered essential to attend if you had any business or political ambitions. Usually Amadou hated this kind of black-tie affair, but Jean-Paul was right. With so many opinion makers in attendance it would be the perfect opportunity to catch their prey, a prominent Parisian with a penchant for importing unsuspecting girls for the sex trade.

Probably neither of them would ever be invited to another formal affair in Paris, but that was just fine with him.

Lina walked out of Louis Vuitton, where she'd just been cajoled into buying a new shoulder bag for Liesel. She wasn't entirely sure how it had happened, but did it really matter? Now Liesel was onto a new urgent want—the big Gaia event Lina rather hoped to avoid.

"You have a ticket already? Why didn't you say so?" Liesel's voice rose to a delighted squeal. "I thought we were going to have to call in a favor. Getting another one for me shouldn't be hard if you're already on the list."

"You can have mine. I was planning to go back to Altaleone that day, anyway." She had no concrete plans yet, but this should throw Liesel off the scent of thinking she had a reason to stay in Paris.

"Nonsense. You can't miss it. Everyone who's anyone will be there."

"I find those events daunting without Emil."

"You'll have me!" Liesel wrapped a skinny arm around her back. "How exciting. We must find something to wear. Is Callista going, too?"

"Yes. Her company bought a table."

"Excellent. She needs to go out and about in order to find a suitable husband. All the crowned heads of Europe will be there."

Lina suppressed a laugh. That was very

unlikely. She knew Darias and Emma weren't coming, for a start. "She's been begging me to go with her."

"We must find her something magnificent to wear."

So by four that afternoon the three of them were shopping for dresses together and Lina found herself in a paroxysm of terror that Callista might somehow mention Amadou and let that cat out of the bag.

Not that Callista knew about anything except that first dinner, of course.

"Amadou Khadem is one of the speakers," proclaimed Callista at last while fondling a cobalt chiffon dress.

Lina froze. "Oh." She tried to sound as nonchalant as possible.

"Oh, God. He's that rock star that's staying at my hotel. What a bore. Cameras everywhere."

"He's not a rock star, Aunt Liesel. His music is fusion. They call it desert soul."

"I don't care what it is. I like some peace and quiet in my hotel lobby."

"Did you know that Mom had dinner with him last week?"

Lina tried to pretend she was fully absorbed in the diamante choker neckline of a slinky green gown.

But she could feel Liesel's fierce gaze boring into her. "What?"

Lina shrugged without looking up. "We're old acquaintances." She hoped her face wasn't heating. She felt like Judas betraying Jesus. "We simply caught up with each other over a bite."

"You are a dark horse, aren't you." Liesel moved in close. "Dinner with a man young enough to be your son. You do know he has girls ogling him everywhere he goes."

"He's actually one year older than Mom," said Callista helpfully. "And I'm one of the girls ogling him. He's gorgeous."

Liesel ignored her. "You should be careful," she said pointedly to Lina. "People will talk."

"No one other than you," said Lina coldly. "What do you think of this one?" She pulled a hideous purple dress with a big ruffle off the rack, hoping it would be enough of a distraction.

"Frightful." Liesel feigned a shudder. "I'm sure Mr. Khadem would love it."

Callista laughed. "Hey, crazy thought, if he's going to the Gaia event and we're going to the Gaia event, why don't we ask him to sit at our table? My boss would be thrilled."

"I don't think so," said Lina, imagining what an utter disaster that would be. She'd have a hard enough time keeping a straight face just watching him up onstage, let alone sitting right across from him. Or worse, next to him. "I'm sure he has someone more important to sit with."

"Mom, I know you like to forget that you are royalty, but you'd be surprised how eager people are to sit with royals. And I could tell he liked you. I'll ask him. I've met him now, after all."

"Do as you please." She pulled out an even more hideous dress with a bold pattern of paint strokes. She couldn't risk protesting too much and giving the game away. She'd just have to leave it up to fate. Surely Amadou would be sensible enough to refuse, even if he didn't have a more important table to sit at. "How about this one?"

Back at her hotel, Lina was exhausted after spending the afternoon shopping and trying not to think about—or talk about—Amadou. Callista had extracted his phone number from her and promised to call him. Now she attempted to watch the French evening news while wondering how he would respond to the invitation.

She didn't have to wait long. She was just about to get in the shower when her phone rang. It was him.

"Hello." She tried to sound bright and casual.

"Hello, beautiful." The way he said it, deep and slow, it didn't sound cheesy. He made her feel beautiful, and not in the "has a skilled dermatologist" way. "Callista called me."

"I know. It was all her idea."

"I had a feeling it was. Don't worry, I made my regrets politely."

Now she felt bad. He was so sure she wouldn't want him to sit with her at a public event. "It would have been fine if you said yes."

"Really?" He sounded so surprised.

"Really. Not that we could kiss or anything, but I don't suppose we have to pretend to be strangers."

His silence spoke volumes. Then he spoke. "That's reassuring to know. But I do have another table I need to sit at. Longtime colleagues. It would be rude if I moved."

Something in his voice suggested that he wasn't telling the full truth.

Would he be there with a woman?

If he was she'd just have to bear it bravely. She had no claim to him. In fact, until just now she'd pretty much let him know they couldn't even be seen together.

"I hear you're one of the speakers."

"Yes." More silence. "I might not even have a chance to say hello, but I don't want you to think it's because I don't want to."

"No worries. I'll have Callista and Liesel to occupy me."

There were three more nights, including tonight, and two days before the party. She had plenty of time to see him again before then.

If he wanted to.

"I'll be very busy over the next couple of days, too. I just wanted you to know I appreciated the invitation, even if it wasn't your idea. Have a good night's sleep."

"You too."

And then he was gone. No attempt to make plans. Not even a hint that he wanted to.

Lina sighed and put her phone down. She'd left the shower running and the bathroom was all steamed up.

So was she.

And now that she was growing rash enough to want to continue their dalliance, he'd gone cold on her.

She probably deserved it.

13

Not a word from Amadou for two days. Nothing on the day of the party, either. Why had he gone so silent?

She decided to take him at his word that he was busy. He was up for a Grammy, after all. He was probably planning his next tour or hashing out the details of a record deal.

She dressed in the sleek, slightly roman-style dress she'd been talked into. It was a weird bronzy-brown color that she would never have chosen for herself, but Callista insisted that it looked fabulous on her. It had little pieces of chain at the shoulders.

Hopefully she didn't look too foolish.

Liesel's driver dropped them off at the venue, a gorgeous château somehow buried in the middle of Paris, and they walked together into the vast ballroom created beneath the glass of a conservatory.

Liesel beamed, taking in the extravagant centerpieces and the formally attired waiters sweeping around with silver trays of champagne glasses. Lina sometimes forgot that she rarely had the opportunity to attend these kinds of events. No wonder her sister was crabby and judgmental. She spent most of her time alone in the remote rural manse they'd grown up in, with only her horses and a small staff for company.

She resolved to make sure that Liesel had a great time and would have plenty to brag about to her friends. If she had any, which was doubtful.

"Let's find our table, then we can mill about and see who's here." She managed to sound excited. As if she hadn't burned out on these extravagant affairs years ago.

Callista looked radiant in a blue gown that contrasted beautifully with her chestnut hair. Maybe they really could find her a nice partner? She spent too much time alone with her work.

But as they milled around, chitchatting with people they knew, Lina found her mind endlessly returning to the subject of Amadou and his whereabouts. Where was he? If she could pinpoint him and his table she could make sure to avoid it and not accidentally glance in that direction and see him with some gorgeous supermodel.

But she didn't see him anywhere. Not in the atrium with the koi pond and the hibachi hors d'oeuvres. Nor in the main ballroom, with its sparkling fountain and endless reserves of champagne, either. Maybe he was in some hidden VIP area for presenters.

When they were summoned to their tables for dinner, she busied herself with meeting Callista's invited guests, sweet young scientists and an older professor of hers. She even realized, with a touch of chagrin, that Callista might have invited the professor as a sort of date for her. He was a handsome man with a gray beard. The kind of guy who probably wore a tweed jacket and a bow tie and made them look chic.

But compared with Amadou? No chance.

She introduced him to Liesel and tried to encourage them into conversation. Maybe her sister would soften up and transform in the hands of the right man.

Unlikely, but you never knew.

The first speaker extolled the virtues of personal sacrifice while they ate an appetizer of Arctic crab. The second speaker—while they picked apart an elaborate roulade—enumerated some of the many wonderful things the Gaia organization had already accomplished that year, including supplying medicines to three different war-torn areas and manufacturing and providing a new design of high-tech tents for refugees.

It was uncomfortably ironic to sit at the table, sipping expensive wine and watching video footage of refugees in their tents. Callista and her young friends were even beginning to get a bit upset or embarrassed about it. Lina knew from decades of experience that this was how they guilt-tripped their captive audience into impressive donations on top of the extortionate ticket price. Brilliant, really.

"Mom, do stop looking so pleased with yourself. This is beyond awkward."

"Looking relaxed is all part of being royal, darling. Did I fail to mention that to you?"

Maybe the champagne and wine were going to her head. She wanted a pleasant buzz going before she had to keep a straight face when Amadou took the stage.

And at long last, just as they spooned up the last of their dessert of sugar-crusted berries and fresh whipped cream, he appeared.

The applause was discreet and muted compared with the kind of enthusiasm she'd witnessed at his concert, but this room of oligarchs and trophy wives was hardly his target audience.

"Ladies and gentlemen…" His speech started out like all the others. He wasn't wearing the usual black-tie attire, though. He had on a high-collared black jacket with no ornamentation whatsoever. He looked more severe than usual, with the spotlight picking out his high cheekbones.

Funny that he hadn't wanted to see her again this week. Maybe he'd already had his fill. He was talking about human trafficking. It really was a litany of the worst of humanity tonight. She'd be sure to give a big donation to his cause, though. Without telling him, of course.

"And tonight we're here to draw attention to the work of one of our esteemed and well-respected guests, seated at table sixteen."

Lina couldn't resist craning her neck to look for table sixteen, and many others did, too. It was hard to tell one table from another, so she gave up and turned back to the stage, where another video had started. This one was different, though. Instead of video images, the screen was black, with chilling statistics about human trafficking in France and in Europe picked out in bold white. This must be a personal cause for him, given his mother's experience.

The audio was odd. Not a narrative. It sounded like a phone conversation. She glanced at Callista, who looked equally confused. Then—steeling herself—she looked at Amadou, whose attention was focused on someone in their seated audience. Possibly the man at table sixteen. She followed his gaze but couldn't see anything as the lights were dimmed.

As the phone conversation continued she realized it was some kind of negotiation over cargo. One of the voices became raised, shouting in French about the previously agreed price and how it wasn't cheap to pay off the police.

On the screen lingered a grim statistic about forced prostitution in Paris.

"I'm telling you, they're all young. Some of them aren't half bad looking. It's just as you ordered."

Heads turned as some kind of scuffle erupted in the direction that Amadou was staring. Suddenly the lights came back on, and Amadou leaned into the microphone. "As you may have discerned the voice you heard was that of Gascoine Monceau, our esteemed Prefect of Police, negotiating the paid-for arrival of a truckload of young girls from the Balkans. Girls intended to serve as prostitutes in a ring of brothels he's been running here in Paris and across northern Europe. Also implicated in the ring—which we have been gathering evidence on for two years—are…" He proceeded to name a prominent politician, a right-wing journalist and the CEO of a large electronics firm.

A hushed whisper had spread through the audience and risen to a roar. At what must be table sixteen, two men in black tie were now firmly holding another formally dressed guest in a kind of armlock. Others rose from their tables, and a sense of chaos erupted throughout the room.

"What's going on?" She turned to Callista, feeling stupid. "I don't understand."

"Me either."

The man being held bellowed about suing and insisting that the recording was fake. People were starting to grab their purses and head for the exits.

"What on earth is going on? We haven't had coffee yet." Liesel looked as confused as they did. "It's that awful man from my hotel. I can't believe you know him. He's just accused several prominent members of society of horrible crimes that they couldn't possibly have committed. He must be mad."

Amadou wasn't on the stage any longer. Lina couldn't see where he'd gone. "Perhaps we'd better go, too."

"There's rather a crush at the exits. Let's wait," said a nice young scientist that Callista had brought. "I'm sure the police will be here to arrest them."

"He is the police." Lina tried to see what was going on, but too many people now stood between her and the infamous table sixteen. "I suppose that's why he had to be accused in a public place with a lot of witnesses."

But why was Amadou the accuser? He must have been in on some plot.

It explained why he hadn't come near her all night. Maybe even why he'd avoided her for the past two days, if he was busy putting this together.

She looked around for him but a sudden crush of uniformed police obscured her view, and there was a lot of yelling that, despite her pretty good French, she couldn't understand. The overhead lights suddenly switched on high, giving the decorated ballroom a gaudy and exposed air.

"The evening is ruined. We need to leave," said Liesel, standing. "Now."

"Are you okay, Mom?" Callista put a hand on her shoulder.

"I'm a bit worried." Where was Amadou in all this crush? As the accuser, in what was presumably a surprise onslaught against an important police figure, he might be in real danger in this crush of uniformed men. "I think we should find him."

"Find who?" Liesel grabbed an extra goody bag from a deserted table and shoved the bottle of expensive scent from it into her purse. "How are we going to get out of here?" The atmosphere in the room now had an undercurrent of panic, with nearly every table abandoned.

"He'll be fine, Mom. I think we'd better go." Callista looked worried, and the young men at their table were hovering protectively. "I'm sure we'll find out what happened in the papers tomorrow. It was obviously planned."

Lina allowed herself to be hustled toward the exit, feeling totally lost. Why hadn't he told her about this? He might have warned her. Obviously he didn't consider her trustworthy enough to be a confidant—and why would he? She'd done her best to keep him at arm's length, and now he'd returned the favor.

It was just what she'd wanted, wasn't it?

14

Lina texted Amadou as soon as she got back to the hotel. Then again two hours later after no response. After a few hours of restless attempts at sleep, she texted him again—nothing—and checked the headlines.

"Police Chief Accused" was the main headline, followed by a confusing mix of information about the event and information that no formal charges had been made. Amadou wasn't even mentioned, which was odd, considering his fame and his prominent role in the accusation.

His absence from the story gave her the creeps. Her silent phone mocked her.

From what she gathered the accused man was part of a large ring with mob connections in the Balkans. Scary and dangerous people. Could someone as well-known as Amadou be made to simply disappear?

Panic had her marching around her room, feeling helpless and useless, when she heard a knock on the door. She was still in her robe and not ready for the maid. "Who is it?"

"It's me." Amadou's unmistakable, deep

voice.

She flew to the door and tugged it open. Words deserted her as she hugged him tight.

"Sorry to surprise you like this. I had no way to get in touch." He kissed her forehead gently.

"Where have you been? I've been texting you."

"The police have my phone. I'm not sure who's in more trouble, me or the scumbags I accused last night. I think it's me." Humor crinkled the skin around his eyes. "I've been told there's a mob hit out for me."

"What?" The door was still open, and she scanned the hallway. Then tugged him inside and locked it.

"And I don't exactly feel like law enforcement is on my side. I'm planning to head out of the country for a while until things settle down. A friend is getting his yacht ready in Montpelier, and we're going to head to the Greek Isles for a while. I didn't want to leave you without saying goodbye."

Goodbye.

The word sent a chill through her. She was fiercely proud of him for the risk he'd taken, but she didn't want to lose him.

"How long will you be in hiding?"

He laughed. "I won't be hiding. I just won't be lining myself up in anyone's crosshairs, either. I have a series of concerts in Japan next month, anyway. Then after that, some gigs in Canada."

"So you'll be on the road." Traveling from city to city. Meeting new women.

"As always." He shrugged, but there was something in his eyes. A glint of fresh emotion. Maybe he was afraid. He'd taken a big risk, and her heart ached for him.

"Will they prosecute the people behind the ring of human traffickers?"

"They'll have to do something. Too many witnesses. Even if the evidence gets thrown out in court for being illegal phone tapping, a lot of important people now know the truth. They could go after them on other grounds. Criminal activities usually involve tax evasion, for example. I'm pretty sure the reason they had me present the information is because they think I am too high profile to just disappear. I didn't want to do it, as I do some work undercover for the same organization, sometimes even pretending to be a trafficker, and now I won't be able to."

"People didn't recognize you before?"

"Out of context, never. Kind of humbling, really."

"It sounds dangerous."

"Living is dangerous."

"Not like that." Then she remembered how her own mild-mannered husband, who never stuck his neck out anywhere, had been murdered in cold blood. "Then again, maybe you're right. I guess we all take a big risk just getting out of bed every day."

"Could get hit by a car." His face creased with the hint of grin.

Her chest ached. She wanted to hold him. Here they were talking about how you could die at any minute, and yet she was holding herself back with all her willpower.

Because he'd come to say goodbye. It might be years before she saw him again, if ever.

The thought made a sob rise inside her, and she choked it back.

His smile had faded, and his features hardened. His eyes grew dark as onyx. "Come with me."

"To Greece?"

"Everywhere."

A nervous laugh escaped. "You know I can't do that."

"Why not?"

Her chest tightened. "My duty to Altaleone. I have responsibilities. My son needs me."

He took her hands. "I need you."

"You've survived without me all this time." He must be taunting her. Wanting her to confess how much she cared, so he could walk coolly away as she'd done all those years ago.

"I never married anyone else. Never wanted to." He raised her hands to his lips and pressed them softly. "Marry me, Lina. It's not too late. We could still share the rest of our lives."

Emotion flooded her, and she rocked on her heels. He must be mad.

And so must she, because the prospect of leaving her settled life swept through her like a tidal wave.

She threw out an anchor. "My husband is barely dead a year. It would be unseemly."

"Who cares?" He pressed his lips together in an attitude of determination. Clearly she was giving him hope. "Do it anyway."

"I can't just…travel around with you everywhere."

"Why not? We can go back to Altaleone, or wherever else you like, as often as we want. I play a few nights, then often have weeks off to do whatever I please."

"Which is apparently interfering with human trafficking rings."

He chuckled. "Yes, but since I'll have to lay low on that for a while I'll have some free time."

He squeezed her hands. The whole idea was so outlandish. But was following him around the world really all that different to becoming a satellite in one of Europe's royal families? She'd walked into her husband's routines, learned his culture and adapted herself to his lifestyle. And been happy. "I do like to travel. And I've never been to Japan."

Amadou's eyes widened slightly. Had he not expected her to be receptive? Maybe he'd backpedal now. "You'd like Kyoto. The ancient gardens show that you can create paradise in miniature here on earth and maintain it carefully for centuries."

"I like the idea of paradise on earth."

"Better than waiting for it in the hereafter." He unfolded her hands, which were almost clenched, then kissed her ring finger. "Will you marry me, Lina? I love you as much as ever, and I want you to be mine and only mine."

A teeny sob escaped her as emotion racked her body. "I love you too, Amadou. I know it sounds terrible, but I'm not sure I ever really stopped loving you. I think I just put it on hold somewhere." That was why her feelings for him had scared her so much that she didn't want to see him again.

"It doesn't sound terrible. Marrying your husband was part of your journey. Your children are a glorious part of that. And I'm sure they won't resent you choosing to be happy now."

A tear trickled over her cheek, and she lifted a hand to brush it away. "Liesel will resent it."

He laughed. "Sounds like another good reason to go for it."

She laughed too, so much tension in her wanting release. "For goodness sake, kiss me."

He obliged, lowering his lips over hers with such tenderness that she thought her heart might explode. He took her in his arms and held her—gently but firmly—and kissed her until she couldn't breathe or think anymore.

When their lips finally parted she'd made up her mind. "I will marry you."

"Yes!" His whoop of victory hurt her ears. "I promise I'll make you happy. I'd take you ring shopping right now, but I think we should wait until we get to Greece."

"Do they have jewelry shops in the Greek Islands?"

"We'll find one somewhere. I think we should get matching rings."

A frightening thought occurred to her. "What about the wedding? Who would we invite? Where would we have it? It seems impossible."

He frowned. "I don't even want one. I just

want to be married to you."

Adrenaline surged through her. "Then let's go find an officiant. We won't even tell anyone until it's done."

"Let me call a friend who knows how these things work."

Less than six hours later they were in the beautiful garden at his mother's house under heavy private security, with his friends Mustafa and Jean-Paul as witnesses, pledging a lifetime of love before the Altaleone ambassador.

Lina wore a silver-white evening dress with silver sandals that she'd bought by herself at Printemps. She hadn't even dared tell Callista about her plans for fear her daughter should throw up some roadblock like insisting on including all her siblings.

Self-assured and confident, Lina needed no one to give her away, and breaking tradition once again, she and Amadou held hands as they recited their heartfelt vows.

Her heart swelled almost to bursting as she said them. "I, Carolina Leone take you, Amadou Khadem, as my husband and promise to love you without reservation, comfort you in times of distress, laugh with you and cry with you, grow with you in mind, and spirit, always be open and honest with you, and cherish you for as long as we both shall live."

Amadou blinked, eyes shining and face taut with emotion. "In this beautiful garden I dedicate myself to you. Although our lives may change like the seasons, I will love you. As our love grows like a seed to a beautiful flower, I will love you. When the winds of doubt blow through, I will love you. We will stand together, strong, nurtured by each other's love until the end."

Their kiss tasted sweeter than ever as it sealed the seed of love that they'd each carried inside them for so long. Lina blinked back tears. "I won't ever leave you again."

"You're damn right you won't." He grinned and squeezed her tight. "I won't let you out of my sight from now on."

EPILOGUE

One month later...

"What do you think of Altaleone so far?" Lina lay with her head on Amadou's chest, the sheets draped loosely over both of them.

"My favorite thing about it is that you're in bed with me here."

She chuckled. He'd strangely dreaded coming here and still seemed somewhat wary walking around the village, despite strangers greeting him with enthusiasm. "It's odd that you'd never been here before, even for one of our spectacular outdoor festivals. Most of the world's music stars have played here at least once."

"I hadn't been here because I was deliberately avoiding the place." She could feel his heart beat, strong and steady, beneath her cheek. "I didn't like that you were here, sharing your life with someone else."

Even now they chose not to stay in the palace. Amadou didn't want to sleep with her in the home she'd shared with her husband. Instead they shared a suite in the old stone castle that Darias and Emma had renovated.

She stroked his stubbled cheek. "It would have been strange to run into you back then. Just imagine."

"You'd have pretended not to know me." His voice was a low growl.

She bit her lip. Would she? Possibly. How mortifying to think about.

"So it's lucky I just kept my distance and patiently waited for you to be free again."

"The way you're talking I almost suspect you of killing him." They both laughed. "And we both know you weren't actually waiting." He'd had well-publicized affairs with plenty of women in the meantime.

"Just biding my time." He kissed the top of her head. "Trying to keep busy."

"While secretly rescuing people from exploitation."

"I was in a unique position to do so because I traveled so much." He'd slowed down a lot, ostensibly because his cover was blown, but also because she didn't like him putting himself in danger. Which was selfish, really.

"With all the evidence that has emerged, prosecutors are confident that the crooked police chief will get at least fifteen years in prison, and four of his cronies are coming up for trial, including the mob boss who supposedly ordered a hit on you."

"I can close both eyes while I sleep now."

"You didn't lose a wink of sleep over this." She pushed his chest playfully.

"I'm not the nervous type."

"I can tell." She put a hand on either side of

his chest. "I find that very relaxing. Can we go to Australia a couple of days early? I've always wanted to try diving on the Great Barrier Reef."

"Don't you want to be here to watch your roses bloom?"

She smiled. "It's sweet of you to remember my roses, but I've seen them bloom twenty times or more. I'm ready for new adventures."

He leaned forward, and she lifted her head to kiss him gently on the lips.

"Me, too. And you know where my favorite place to dive is?"

"No, where?" She eased herself up on the bed until she was level with him, one arm draped over his hard stomach.

"Tahiti."

"I've never been there, either."

"Hey, why don't we rent a villa there and invite all your kids to join us?"

"That's a great idea. And we could invite your mom."

"She'd never try to dive, but she does enjoy sitting under a palm tree. She hates to fly though. I have to fly with her."

"We can pass through Paris on the way and pick her up. Maybe she and I can do a little shopping first." Paris was now their second home. It was strange how easily she'd transitioned into her new life. And hard to imagine how she'd been happy with such a quiet and circumscribed existence before.

"Sounds like a plan. But first I have other plans." He dragged an elegant yet powerful finger down over her torso, circled her belly button, then trailed it lower.

"Oh, really?" She lifted a brow as her insides quivered. The sheets shifted where his arousal moved them. "Are you sure we can fit your plans in before dinner with Darias and Emma? The Swiss ambassador and his wife are coming tonight."

"I can manage," he rasped, already closing his mouth over hers. Then he took charge of her body the way he'd taken charge of her life— filling them both with pleasure and joy beyond her wildest imaginings.

THE END

The complete Royal House of Leone Series:
The King's Bought Bride (Darias and Emma)
A Prince for Christmas (Sandro and Serena)
The Prince's Secret Baby (Sandro and Serena)
The Princess and the Player (Lina and Amadou)
The Princess's Scandalous Affair (Beatriz and
Lorenzo)
Taming the Royal Beast (Rigo and Bella)

For more information visit www.jenlewis.com.

ABOUT THE AUTHOR

Jennifer Lewis loves heat in all its forms including spicy food, steamy temperatures and smoking hot heroes. She is a USA TODAY bestselling author and her books have been translated into more than twenty languages. She lives in sunny South Florida and when she's not sitting at her laptop she can often be found at the beach. Read more about her books and join her new release mailing list at www.jenlewis.com.

www.ingramcontent.com/pod-product-compliance
Lightning Source LLC
Chambersburg PA
CBHW020409130626
46549CB00006B/2491